INDEPENDE
THE DORSET BOY

This is a work of Fiction. All characters and stories are fictional although based in historical settings. If you see your name appear in the story, it is a coincidence, or maybe I asked first.

All rights reserved. No part of this book may be reproduced, stored in a retrieval system or transmitted in any form by any means electronic, mechanical, photocopying, recording or otherwise, except brief extracts for the purpose of review, nor used to train AI systems, programs or Applications without the permission of the copyright owner.

Copyright © 2024 Christopher C Tubbs

Acknowledgements

Thanks to Dawn Spears the brilliant artist who created the cover artwork and my editor Debz Hobbs-Wyatt without whom the books wouldn't be as good as they are.

My wife, Jo, who manages my social media content, is so supportive and believes in me. Lastly, our dog Blaez and cats Vaskr and Rosa who watch me act out the fight scenes and must wonder what the hell has gotten into their boss. And a special thank you to Troy who was the grandfather of Blaez in real life. He was a magnificent beast just like his grandson!

THANK YOU FOR READING!

I hope you enjoy reading this book as much as I enjoyed writing it. Reviews are so helpful to authors. I really appreciate all reviews, both positive and negative. If you want to leave one, you can do so on Amazon, through my website, or on Twitter.

www.thedorsetboy.com

#ChristopherCTu3

About the Author

Christopher C Tubbs is a dog-loving descendent of a long line of Dorset clay miners and has chased his family tree back to the 16th century in the Isle of Purbeck. He left school at sixteen to train as an Avionics Craftsman, has been a public speaker at conferences for most of his career and was one of the founders of a successful games company back in the 1990s. Now in his sixties, he finally writes the stories he had been dreaming about for years. Thanks to inspiration from great authors like C S Forester, Alexander Kent, Dewey Lambdin, Patrick O'Brian, Raymond E Feist and Dudley Pope, he was finally able to put digit to keyboard. He lives in the Netherlands Antilles with his wife, two Dutch Shepherds, and two Norwegian Forest cats.

You can visit him on his website
www.thedorsetboy.com
The Dorset Boy, Facebook page.

Or tweet him @ChristopherCTu3

The Dorset Boy Series Timeline

1792 – 1795   Book 1: A Talent for Trouble.
Marty joins the navy as an assistant steward and through a series of adventures ends up a midshipman.

1795 – 1798   Book 2: The Special Operations Flotilla.
Marty is a founder member of the Special Operations Flotilla, learns to be a spy and passes as Lieutenant.

1799 – 1802   Book 3: Agent Provocateur.
Marty teams up with Linette to infiltrate Paris, marries Caroline, becomes a father and fights pirates in Madagascar.

1802 – 1804   Book 4: In Dangerous Company.
Marty and Caroline are in India helping out Arthur Wellesley, combating French efforts to disrupt the East India Company and French-sponsored pirates on Reunion. James Stockley was born.

1804 – 1805   Book 5: The Tempest.
Piracy in the Caribbean, French interference, Spanish gold and the death of Nelson. Marty makes Captain.

1806 – 1807   Book 6: Vendetta.

A favour carried out for a prince, a new ship, the SOF move to Gibraltar, the battle of Maida, counter espionage in Malta and a Vendetta declared and closed.

1807 – 1809   Book 7: The Trojan Horse.

Rescue of the Portuguese royal family, Battle of the Basque Roads with Thomas Cochrane, and back to the Indian Ocean and another conflict with the French Intelligence Service.

1809 – 1811   Book 8: La Licorne.

Marty takes on the role of Viscount Wellington's Head of Intelligence. Battle of The Lines of Torres Vedras, siege of Cadiz, skulduggery, espionage and blowing stuff up to confound the French.

1812   Book 9: Raider.

Marty is busy. From London to Paris to America and back to the Mediterranean for the battle of Salamanca. A mission to the Adriatic reveals a white-slavery racket that results in a private mission to the Caribbean to rescue his children.

1813 – 1814   Book 10: Silverthorn

Promoted to Commodore and given a viscountcy. Marty is sent to the Caribbean to be Governor of Aruba which provides the cover story he needs to fight American privateers and undermine the Spanish in South America. On his return, he escorts Napoleon into Exile on Alba.

1815 – 1816   Book 11: Exile

After 100 days in exile, Napoleon returns to France and Marty tries to hunt him down. After the battle of Waterloo Marty again escorts him into exile on St Helena. His help is requested by the governor of Ceylon against the rebels in Kandy.

1817 – 1818   Book 12: Dynasty

To Paris to stop an assassination, then the Mediterranean to further British interests in the region. Finally, to Calcutta as Military Attaché to take part in the war with the Maratha Empire. Beth comes into her own as a spy, but James prefers the navy life.

1818 -- 1819   Book 13: Empire

The end of the third Anglo-Maratha war and the establishment of the Raj. Intrigue in India, war with the Pindaris, the foundation of Singapore, shipwreck, sea wars and storms.

1820 - 1821   Book 14: Revolution

The Ottoman Empire is starting to disintegrate. The Greeks are starting to revolt. Marty has a promise to keep so Britain can gain Cyprus. Just to complicate things King John of Portugal needs his support as well.

1822 -1824   Book 15: Burma

The 1st Anglo-Burma war is looming, and the East India Company and the British government need an excuse to start it. Marty is sent to Burma as Ambassador to get things moving.

1830-1831   Book 16: Independence

The Greeks are getting ever closer to Independence and the Turks offer the Egyptians the country if they can take it. Atrocities follow, forcing the British, French and Russians to intervene.

Contents

The Navy Way

Rear Admiral Martin Stockley, Viscount Purbeck, stepped down from his carriage in front of Admiralty House. The building designed by Thomas Ripley was U-shaped and made of red brick. It would have been rather plain if not for the screen that covered the entrance designed by Robert Adam at the end of the previous century. As it was, Marty had to walk through the grand Purbeck stone entrance into the courtyard.

The summons from the First Lord of the Admiralty, Robert Dundas, had arrived the day before by navy courier and simply said he had to present himself to the first lord at eleven in the morning the following day. It was a quarter to eleven as Marty stepped into the foyer and was greeted by the appointments clerk.

"Admiral, good morning, you can go straight up. The first lord is expecting you."

"Thank you, Chivers."

He cast an eye over the crowd of midshipmen and lieutenants all looking for a berth on a ship.

"Good morning, gentlemen."

They all stood and touched a forelock, some, mainly the younger ones, gaping in awe at the famous admiral.

Marty knew the way to the great man's office and timed his approach to perfection, knocking on the door at precisely eleven o'clock.

"Come."

He entered and saw that Dundas was not alone.

"Good morning, Milord. Good morning, Arthur."

The Duke of Wellington, Arthur Wellesley, stood and shook his hand.

Arthur gave one of his half smiles.

"Good morning."

Marty took the seat indicated and looked at them in turn.

"If both of you are here then I am either in real trouble or you have something difficult for me to do."

Dundas nodded.

"Very astute, Admiral, I can assure you have done nothing to warrant our intervention. On the contrary you have performed impeccably."

Arthur leaned forward.

"You have had a large influence on the progress the Greeks have made towards independence to date. It is unfortunate that they seem to be incapable of working together as a nation to make it stick. Further to that there has been, up to now, little will on the part of the Congress of Nations to support them."

Marty sat back and looked at him as what he said sunk in.

"Until now?"

"Russia, France and Britain are negotiating a new accord, The Treaty of London, that calls for a cessation of hostilities and supports the Greek's right to self-government as part of the Ottoman Empire. The three nations will mediate the agreement."

Marty interjected.

"That's very good, but have the Ottomans and the Greeks agreed to it?"

Dundas answered.

"Not yet, but the Greeks will when they find out that the Ottomans have enlisted the aid of Egypt and Algeria with a promise to enslave any Greeks they capture."

Arthur continued, "The Greeks are under the misapprehension that they have a superior navy to the Ottomans. It's commanded by your old friend Cochrane."

Marty pursed his lips, fingers steepled in front of his mouth.

"The addition of Egyptian and Algerian ships will create an armada with enough troops to subjugate entire regions."

"Exactly," the two statesmen agreed.

"So, what do you want me to do?"

Dundas gave him a faint smile.

"You, my friend, are being given command of the Mediterranean fleet and will be in overall command of the force of British, Russian and French ships we will assemble to stop that armada in its tracks."

Marty looked surprised and Arthur chuckled.

"Who better? Welcome back to the real navy."

"Your orders," Dundas said and handed him an exceptionally thick packet. He stood and went to a sideboard where a tantalus and glasses stood. He poured three glasses of brandy and handed them around.

"Here is to the success of your first fleet command."

They raised their glasses and drained them to heel taps.

**

Marty sat in his study in their Grosvenor Square house and read his orders. They were wrapped up in all the usual fluff that admiralty orders always were and warned of failure at his peril. However, the meat of it was he was to proceed to Portsmouth and join His Majesty's Ship Asia, an eighty-four-gun second rate, which would be his flagship, and proceed to Malta along with the third rates, Genoa and Albion, and the fifth-rate Glasgow. They would join the Ionian squadron of two fifth rates, a sixth-rate, a sloop, three brig sloops and a cutter.

He read on. The Russians were expected to send eight ships including a second rate and the French seven including a second rate. It would be quite a force with probably nine or ten liners of third rate or higher and the rest frigates or smaller.

The Ottomans were expected to assemble an armada of at least ninety ships.

I'm damned if we don't have them outnumbered!

There was a knock at the door. He folded the orders and slipped them into a leather document case.

"Come in."

Adam opened the door and led a navy lieutenant into the room. He wore the gold braid of a flag officer and stood at attention in front of Marty.

"Relax, Lieutenant. What can I do for you?"

The lieutenant looked to be in his late twenties, fair haired, fine featured, broad of shoulder and slim of waist. An inch taller than Marty. He held out a packet.

"My orders, Sir."

Marty took them and went to the chair behind his desk and sat while he read them.

"Jeremy Grandholm. You have been sent to me as my flag lieutenant. I see you served under Pellew as a mid and on the Cumberland as the fourth. Since then, you have been at the admiralty."

"Aye, Sir."

Marty caught the smell of interest.

"Why you?"

"My father asked the first lord to get me somewhere I could see some action."

"And who is your father?"

"It is easier to say that the first lord is my great uncle by marriage."

"I see."

"Well, I will be leaving for Portsmouth the day after tomorrow. Be here by six thirty in the morning with your sea chest. Do not be late as it's a long walk. Until then you can have a last day of freedom in London."

What Marty didn't say was, that a favour given meant a favour owed. Either the father or the first lord would have to pay.

**

Caroline was, as usual, resigned to losing her husband for months if not years at a time and made sure he would remember that he had a wife while he was away. Not with a portrait, although she did give him a new one for his cabin, but by her actions. He got little sleep that night.

A concentrated shopping trip was called for the next day and a sleepy Marty was taken by an invigorated Caroline to buy furniture for his cabin, pick up the uniforms that had been refitted, and order private stores to be delivered directly to the ship. Fortnum and Mason did a brisk trade that day.

Marty had another busy night and was up an hour before dawn. Caroline slept on as was her privilege. Adam and the rest of the Shadows were ready, sea bags already loaded into the second wagon. Adam had packed for Marty and was supervising the loading of his chests including a large iron-bound one that held his weapons. It was battle scarred and showed the signs of travelling around the world; corners scuffed, and wood dented, but he wouldn't be without it.

Caroline appeared as he wolfed down a good breakfast of poached eggs, bacon, black pudding, sausages, kidneys and toast. All washed down with strong Jamaican coffee from their own plantation. A sack of which was already on the wagon.

Caroline grimaced at the sight of the mound of food in front of him.

"How you can eat like that at this time of the morning is beyond me."

"It is a long way to Portsmouth."

"And you will no doubt stop for a hearty lunch. You will get fat."

"I will be grateful for a little extra when we are at sea and the personal stores run out."

Marty mopped up the egg yolk and bacon fat on his plate with a slice of toast, burped, then sighed contentedly.

"The last good breakfast until I return."

He stood and looked at his watch. It was a quarter after six. He was about to say something when there was a knock at the door.

"Come in!" Caroline called.

It was Lieutenant Grandholm.

Marty looked him over; his uniform was impeccable.

"Good morning, Jeremy."

"Good morning, Sir." His nose twitched at the smell of the food.

"Have you breakfasted?" Marty asked.

"No, Sir,"

"Then help yourself, you have ten minutes."

Marty and Caroline left him to it.

Goodbyes said, all that was left was one last hug and an extended kiss, before Marty climbed into the coach. As was his privilege as the senior officer, he was the last to board.

**

The trip to Portsmouth was expedited by a change of horses every ten miles, but even so would take two and a half days. Marty spent the time getting to know his flag lieutenant.

He discovered he had been signed up as a midshipman in '10 at the tender age of ten. He had served aboard Pellew's flagship as a mid in the Mediterranean and was familiar with the western end from Gibraltar to Malta. His service as the fourth on the Cumberland had been after the war from '21 to '24 when his father had wangled him a position at the admiralty. When he heard that Marty was taking over the eastern Mediterranean, he nagged his father into asking his uncle to get him transferred to Marty's staff. As Marty didn't have any, the vacancy was easily filled.

"I suppose it was fate, Sir. This is your first fleet command, and you need a flag lieutenant. I was in the right place at the right time."

"What do you know about me?"

"You have had a, might I say, colourful career both at sea and on land. I must say you have one of the largest files at the admiralty. Only Cochrane has a bigger one."

"Tom would like that. He is in Greece helping them with their navy."

"You know him, don't you, Sir?"

"I do, we fought together at the Basque Roads. It was his last action before he was thrown out of the navy. I hope to see him again if he is still in Greece"

They talked of other things and Marty was surprised by what the young man knew of him, but he had the feeling there was something he still wanted to ask.

At lunch the second day he finally got around to it.

"Sir, may I ask, your followers, It appears they are more than servants?"

"Oh, so that's what's bothering you."

"Well, they are awfully well armed for servants, Sir."

Adam was sat next to Marty and grinned when Marty indicated he should answer.

"I am Milord's valet and steward; I am also a sharpshooter and a member of the Shadows. Antton is the de-facto leader of the Shadows,

Garai is an expert in surveillance, getting into locked places and a knife fighter, Matai is our medic, a formidable fighter and animal handler, Chin is an expert in all forms of combat and climbing, Sam is milord's cox and our muscle and Roland is milord's chef and our explosives expert. Oh, and I almost forgot Hector, personal guard and fighter."

Hector, who was snoozing on the floor of the carriage by Marty's feet, looked up and gave Adam a doggy smile.

Marty elaborated.

"The Shadows are my Special Operations Team."

**

They arrived in Portsmouth and saw their ship moored in the upper harbour alongside the other ships of his embryonic fleet. Sam whistled up several boats and the Shadows loaded the baggage in two, themselves into another and left the fourth to Martin, Sam, Hector and the flag lieutenant.

The Asia was a two-deck second rate built in Bombay and launched in January '24. She was made of teak and armed with:

- Twenty-eight thirty-two-pound cannon and two, sixty-eight-pound carronades on the gundeck.
- Thirty-two twenty-four pounders on the upper gundeck.
- Six twenty-four pounders and ten thirty-two pounders on the quarterdeck.
- Two twenty-four-pounders and four thirty-two-pound carronades.

The admiral's quarters were on the upper gundeck and consisted of a night cabin, day cabin and dining room. They were spacious and, by navy standards, quite luxurious. His few extra items would personalise the space.

Hector had to be lifted aboard in a sling. The mastiff cross shepherd weighed a healthy two hundred pounds now he was fully grown and even Sam couldn't carry that up the battens around the tumblehome. Once aboard and freed he explored and christened the mainmast.

Marty climbed the battens and as his head cleared the deck there was the crash of marines coming to attention, slamming their rifle butts onto the deck, and the shrill song of the bosun's pipes. Captain Edward Curzon and Commander Robert Lambert Baynes stood ready to greet him. As his feet hit the deck he raised his hat to the quarterdeck.

"Welcome aboard the Asia, Admiral," Curzon said and shook Marty's hand. "May I introduce my officers?"

Marty scanned the rigging, seeing a ship in good order.

"Please go ahead, I won't promise to remember all their names immediately though."

Lieutenant Commander Baynes was the first lieutenant, and he was followed by eight lieutenants in descending order of seniority. Finally came the master, thirty-five-year-old Thomas Cleethorpes. Marty thanked the gods that the nineteen midshipmen were not presented.

Marty presented his flag lieutenant and introduced Hector to them all, as the dog came over and sniffed each man, as he shook Marty's hand.

At the end of the formal greeting Curzon noticed the Shadows (less Adam and Roland who had already gone down to the admiral's rooms).

"Your followers, Sir?"

"Yes, Sam, the big one, is my cox. The rest, for the purposes of this posting, can be classified as that."

Curzon looked puzzled so Marty elaborated.

"You know I am part of Naval Intelligence?"

"Yes, I was informed by the first lord."

"They are my personal Special Operations Team. They are all rated able by the way."

Curzon decided he knew enough. At best he had gained a few good hands, at worst they would eat and not be useful.

**

When he got below, Marty found a marine sentry in place. The man stamped to attention and bellowed, "Sah!"

Marty looked at him calmly then leaned in and spoke quietly.

"I have very good hearing. I would be most grateful if you didn't bellow so loudly. Knock on the door, crack it open and tell me who is waiting in a normal voice. Understood?"

The man took a deep breath then thought about it.

"Yes, Sah," he said at a normal volume.

"Good, please inform your colleagues and we will get along famously."

Adam and Roland had been busy. They had found the stewards designated for the admiral's cabin and put them to work unpacking his sea chests and getting his furniture and odds and sods in place. His swords and rifles were in their rack. Caroline's portrait in place over the sideboard, his weapons chest beside the sideboard against the hull.

There were three, twenty-four-pound guns in his quarters. One in each cabin and one in the dining room. These were tied down out of the way and would be hauled into position when the ship went to quarters. At that time the cabin partition walls would be removed, and the furniture and his belongings taken below making the upper gundeck run continuously from stem to stern.

Adjacent to his dining room was a steward's pantry and a kitchen where his personal chef could prepare his food. These were respectively Adam and Roland's domains. His personal stores were in a separate room on the orlop deck. The resident chief steward didn't like it that Adam had usurped him and felt he had lost face. He went to his captain.

"What is it, Merriweather?" Curzon said after granting him an audience.

"I wish to be removed from the admiral's staff, Sir."

"And why is that?"

"He has his own steward, Sir."

"Ahh, I see. Well, the admiral anticipated that. His man is his valet, his gentleman's gentleman, he is not navy and not a steward."

"Not a steward? Well, he's all over my pantry."

Curzon held his temper; this was distracting him from getting his paperwork done and the man was impertinent.

"Although you should not be bothering me with this, I will advise you. Talk to his man and find out what his lordship requires him to do and what you should do. I will not move you to another position so make the best of it."

He went back to his paperwork. Meriweather was dismissed. Back in the pantry he found Adam preparing coffee using an apothecary's pressure vessel.

"There you are," Adam said, wondering at the sour look. "I was going to show you how to operate this. Milord likes his coffee prepared just so."

Curiosity got the better of him.

"Why not make it by pouring water over the grounds?"

"He tells me doing it this way creates more heat and extracts more flavour from the beans. The ship's physician on the Unicorn came up with the method."

The machine hissed and whistled.

"There it is done." Adam blew out the spirit burner and gently turned a valve to let out steam. "You have to reduce the pressure inside carefully or you can get burnt. When it stops spurting you can open it."

The steam trickled to a stop, and he undid the clamps that held the vessel shut. The smell of coffee permeated the room and drifted down the gundeck. He transferred the contents to a silver coffee pot via a strainer and put the pot on a tray with three cups, milk and sugar.

"Three cups?"

"The master and the flag are with him. Here you are, all yours. During the day it's your job to take care of the usual chief steward's duties. I will only take over in the evening."

"You mean I only have to work in the day?"

"Yes, I will take care of his clothes, weapons and personal needs. He doesn't ask for much in the evenings so I can take care of him then, unless he has dinner guests, when we will both be needed."

Merriweather suddenly felt foolish. He had bothered the captain for no reason. He picked up the tray and took it in.

That night the admiral entertained the captains from the fleet: Walter Bathurst of the third-rate Genoa, John Acworth of the third-rate Albion, James Ashley of the fifth-rate Glasgow and Gawen Hamilton of the fifth-rate Cambrian. Rolland prepared a feast of epic quality and sophistication that would have done Antoine Carême proud.

**

The next morning Marty, Jeremy and the master were sat poring over charts, journals and logs. A delivery of coffee interrupted them for just a minute, then they went right back to it.

"The logical place for them to assemble is in the Bay of Navarino. It is big enough for a fleet of that size to gather and be sheltered from any storms," the master said. "It's also protected at either end by castles."

Marty studied the chart that the master had made on a visit ten years ago. "What are these castles like?"

"I described them in my journal." He picked up a volume and leafed through it.

There was a knock at the door, and it opened a crack.

"The captain, Admiral," the marine said.

"Thank you, Jones, show him in."

Curzon entered and took off his hat.

"We are ready to sail, Admiral. May I have my master back?"

"Oh, I'm sorry, Captain, we were engrossed in his records of the Peloponnese. Off you go Thomas."

Jeremy coughed discreetly.

"Admiral, the men expect to see you on deck when we leave port."

Marty sighed and looked across at Adam who held up his uniform coat.

"You are right."

He allowed Adam to help him get into full uniform, buckle on his sword belt and give him his hat. Jeremy led him up to the quarterdeck, where preparations to sail were underway. The ships had been towed to the ammunition dock first thing and taken on their tons of powder. Now they sat above their anchors ready to sail.

Curzon stepped up and touched his hat in salute.

"The preparatory is raised, we will execute at your command, Admiral."

Marty cast an appreciative eye over the Asia and the other ships in his care.

"Get us underway, line astern, Asia leads."

This was as per the briefing over the captains over dinner.

The execute flew up the mast and sails boomed as they took the breeze. The anchor broke loose as the stamp of the men on the capstans shuddered through the deck planking. Marty looked up and at the top of the main mast flew his pennant and command flag.

Command

The Asia made way, the captain had command of the ship and was ably assisted by his officers. Marty had never commanded a ship of the line and he watched with interest as the big ship was manoeuvred out of the harbour. At slow speed the rudder had little effect so most of the steering was achieved through handling the jibs and spanker. The men reacted immediately to commands with no need for starting. Well trained and professional from the landsmen to the topmen, this was a crack crew.

Marty looked astern; they were followed by the Genoa, Albion, Glasgow and Cambrian in that order. He scanned to starboard and saw they were passing Burrow Island and Weevil Lake. Gosport came up and a flag dipped in salute.

They gradually accelerated and Southsea Castle passed on the port side. They were out, and as they swung west Marty let the frigates loose to take position ahead and to either side of the liners.

He turned to the captain.

"Nicely done, I am impressed with your crew. I will be in my cabin if you need me."

**

Marty went through the entries and drawings in the master's journal that described the castles at either end of Navarino Bay. The southern one was newer and built to withstand artillery with sloping, thick walls and bastions. Two of the bastions covered the entrance to the bay and the harbour. An estimated sixty guns covered the walls and ten years ago they were twenty-four pounders.

The northern fortress was much older, dating back to the 13th century and sat on a six-hundred-foot high rock formation. It had been built by the crusaders and resembled a medieval castle. The master had visited it and described it as 'run down with crumbling walls'. The channel was silted and not navigable by anything bigger than a punt.

**

The days passed. Marty had little to do which did not suit his nature. He had researched all he could about Navarino Bay and other less likely locations, worked out how he would blockade them with or without the French ships and re-read his orders at least five times.

He blew out his cheeks and went to the shelf to fetch a book then changed his mind, took off his waistcoat and necktie, opened the top two buttons of his shirt and went to the rack of swords. He selected his favourite hanger and slid his fighting knife into the sheath on the back of his belt.

"Adam!"

Adam appeared a moment later, "Yes, Milord?"

"Tell the boys to meet me on the main deck for weapons practice."

With a completely straight face Adam replied, "They are already waiting for you."

Marty gave him a suspicious look.

"Who won the bet?"

Adam checked his watch. "Garai."

"Get your sword, you need exercise, you're getting chubby."

Adam grinned, he was in excellent shape and knew it.

**

Captain Curzon looked at the admiral in astonishment as he came onto the main deck.

"What the ...." he said, and Baynes joined him.

"What is he doing?"

The Shadows got up from where they were longing and formed a circle around Marty. He spoke to them, and they paired off.

"They are moving stuff, are they clearing that area?"

"I think they are."

"Should I go and ask him what he is doing?"

Curzon looked thoughtful; his admiral was an odd egg.

"No, let's see what he does next."

The men produced weapons and proceeded to fight. The admiral had paired up with the Chinaman who had a pair of swords. They started to fence. Not in the traditional way but as if they were really trying to kill each other.

"My God!" Baynes gasped.

The fight got faster and faster, the swords scintillating in the weak sunshine, the men circling, ducking, and spinning as they fought. A crowd of onlookers formed and work on the ship ground to a halt.

Curzon's attention shifted to two of the other men who were fighting with knives. They were moving so fast that at one point they were almost a blur. The admiral's cox and steward had faced off with staves and went at each other with such vigour he was sure that one would suffer a broken crown.

The fight between the admiral and Chinaman abruptly stopped when the men froze. The admiral's sword point resting on the other's chest. The two men stepped apart and bowed.

"Remind me not to challenge him to a duel," Curzon said.

"We both could and not stand a chance. What are they up to now?"

The admiral moved to a stay and pulled on a pair of gloves; the rangy Basque called Antton took the stay on the other side. The cox called, "Go!" and the two men started to climb.

Baynes was open mouthed in astonishment.

"They are only using their arms!"

Curzon looked on in admiration. Even his fittest topmen would have a hard time keeping up with the two middle-aged men. The Basque won and the two slid to the deck laughing. The others all raced and then the winners faced off against each other until there were only two left. The winner, just, was another of the Basques whose name he didn't know.

The admiral walked up to the quarterdeck. He was sweating but looked happy.

"Nothing like a good exercise session to get the blood flowing."

"Should we expect this every day, Sir?" Curzon asked.

The admiral looked down at the Shadows who were chatting and laughing.

"A weapons training session every day might do the crew some good as well."

Baynes had a vision of gutted and slashed men.

"With live blades?"

The admiral looked somewhat mischievous.

"Oh no, we don't want injuries. Practice swords only. I'll be below."

He disappeared down the steps.

"Well, I'm damned, whoever heard of such a thing," Baynes said.

"Not a bad idea though. Schedule weapons training for the off-duty watches for an hour a day and ask the admiral's men to be the instructors."

**

They stopped at Gibraltar to rendezvous with the rest of the Mediterranean Fleet and Marty got a surprise. His son's ship, the Talbot, was there. He had completely forgotten he had been posted to the Mediterranean Squadron. Along with the Talbot, which was a twenty-eight-gun, sixth-rate frigate, were the Dartmouth, a fifth-rate frigate of forty-two guns, three brig sloops and a cutter. He had hoped the Special Operations Flotilla would be there, but they were working with the Greek Navy.

The smaller ships would be useful for running messages but not much good in a knock down fight between the two fleets. He would have to rely on the fifth and third rates for that. Rapid, aimed fire was the order of the day and he decided that all his ships would need to be brought up to standard.

He called an all-captains meeting to be followed by dinner.

"Gentlemen, we are about to enter into conflict with the Ottomans, Egyptians and Algerians. Our allies in this venture will be the Russians and the French." A muttering started at the mention of the French. Marty held up his hands.

"Yes, gentlemen, the French. Now I understand that working with them rather than blowing them to hell will be somewhat strange, but politics change faster than the wind in a hurricane."

The men laughed, peace with the French was one thing but working with them was an entirely different proposition. They were the old enemy and distrust ran deep.

"I want our gunnery and sail handling to be at their peak by the time we reach the Ionian Sea so we will embark on a rigorous training schedule as soon as we sail." Marty didn't say it, but he wanted his 'allies' to know that the Royal Navy had not lost any of its teeth during the peace.

Several of the captains looked a little worried by his statement. He assumed that they were the ones who had let things slip in the intervening years. The navy still had its share of officers who had gotten their commands through interest and not merit. He decided to up the pressure.

"I will place monitors on your ships to get independent evaluations of the state of readiness after the first two days of training and every two days after that. If any ship is not coming up to the standard that the navy expects then I will shift my flag to that ship to ensure it does."

There were a lot of glances and raised eyebrows exchanged. Their new admiral was living up to his reputation.

**

Business completed, drinks were served by the stewards and a bevy of midshipmen. Marty cast an eye over them. He had discovered that the oldest was twenty years old and had failed his lieutenant's exam twice.

The chances of his being made one now were negligible. The other eighteen ranged in age from twelve to seventeen. The newest was the son of a captain and had joined in Portsmouth. The oldest would be sitting his lieutenant's exam in the next year or so.

He took a glass of Madeira, sipped it and chatted to the captains. James was keeping his distance, but Marty pulled him into a conversation with Thomas Fellows of the Dartmouth and the Honourable William Anson, Commander of the Brig-Sloop Brisk. Anson was the son of Thomas Anson, 2nd Viscount Anson and navy blood ran thick in his veins.

"James, I trust you are enjoying your command?"

"Very much so, she is a fine ship, Sir."

"I think I was as surprised as you were when Dundas told me what he intended." He turned to Fellows. "Dartmouth is a forty-two I believe."

"She is, Sir. A taught ship and fine sailor."

"I know your father. He is King George's physician."

"Yes, he is, he has mentioned you as a friend of the king's."

Marty just smiled.

"You have served under Pellew in the East Indies as well as some time in the West Indies I believe."

"You know me better than most, Milord. I must say I am looking forward to sailing under you. Your reputation is enviable."

Marty caught a glimpse of James rolling his eyes at the flagrant sucking up. He turned to Anson.

"What guns does the Brisk carry?"

"Four long nines and six thirty-two-pound carronades, Sir," the young lieutenant commander said blushing.

"Excellent, I like the mix of longs and carronades. You need to be able to hit at range as well as get in close. A small ship can discomfort the biggest of ships if she is sailed well and uses her guns sensibly."

He finally turned to James.

"The Talbot is armed with carronades, isn't she?"

"Twenty thirty-two-pounders, six eighteens and two long nines as fore chasers, Sir. A fine sailor, fast and stable."

"How fast can your men fire?"

James knew what his father was up to and noted that most of the captains were listening in.

"The carronades can fire every sixty seconds and the long nines every ninety seconds."

"That is the Nelson standard and the one all my ships will be measured by." Marty smiled.

He excused himself and moved on to talk to another group of captains.

**

Adam rang the gong for dinner. The men filed into the dining room and arranged themselves by order of rank and seniority. Curzon and Bathurst sat to Marty's right and left respectively then Acworth and Ashley, Hamilton and Fellows, James and Davies (of the sloop Rose), Anson and Martin (of the Brig Sloops Brisk and Musquito) and finally Chetwynd-Talbot (Brig-Sloop Philomel) and Midshipman Grant (of the Cutter, Hind).

Rolland had sourced some nice ripe tomatoes from ashore and had created a rich tomato soup swirled with thick cream and flavoured with herbs. The captains had never tasted the like.

That was followed by pan-fried turbot on a bed of clams and mussels in a white wine, cream and saffron sauce delicately flavoured with shallots and garlic.

The meat course was roast pork. A whole six-month-old piglet was spit roasted until the skin was crisp and golden and brought to the table whole for Marty to carve. It was served with a sage and onion stuffing, new potatoes, fresh buttered carrots and greens. The accompanying gravy was made with the juices that dripped from the pork into a pan. The fat was removed, and flour added to thicken it and while that was cooking out the bottom of the pan was scraped to get all the stick bits off the bottom. White wine was added and the whole boiled until it was cooked through.

"My Lord, who is your chef? This is like nothing I have ever tasted before!" Fellows exclaimed after devouring the main course.

"That would be Roland. He is one of my followers and has been with me since I was a midshipman. He is a cordon bleu chef and a disciple of Antoine Carême."

The desert was a delicate fruit tart. Coffee, nuts, brandy and port finished off the meal. Midshipman Grant made the royal toast as was customary. The captains went back to their own ships satisfied and a little tipsy.

Honing the Blade

The Fleet left the Straits of Heracles and entered the Mediterranean. The Ganges ran up the signal *10, A* and fired a gun. This was the warning that they should expect evolutions and was passed down the line. Marty then asked for *F, 4* to be flown. This demanded that the liners form a line of battle in the order Genoa, Albion, Asia, followed by the frigates Glasgow, Dartmouth and Cambrian. The sloop Rose was to move up the line to windward and position herself two cables off the Genoa's beam. The rest of the brig sloops were to position themselves off of the third, fifth and seventh ships in the line. The Rose was kept out of the way two cables to windward of the last of the windward screen.

This formation was intended for fighting a force in open water. The liners would engage the enemy line and the screen would initially make sure no ships could attack from windward but later board and capture any enemy ships that were disabled by sailing through the British line if necessary. Marty wanted his officers to be bold. He had little time for timid or cautious men. He intended to instil a sense of 'can do' into all of them.

It was a shambles. He sent them back to their original positions and made them do it again. After the third time he reverted to some standard sail evolutions as he deemed they were just not good enough. He demanded speed and precision and gradually he started to get it.

Gunnery followed, starting with rate of fire. He had lain down the standard and expected them to meet it. Albion and Cambrian drew for last place and the reports from the monitors told why. Both had treated the peace as an excuse to relax and the men had not had gunnery drill for quite some time. That was not to say that the others were perfect. Oh no.

Marty had the whole fleet heave to and had the captain's report aboard.

"Gentlemen, this is not good enough. Some of your gunners couldn't hit a cow's ass with a paddle. Your sail handling is improving but still nowhere near good enough. Consequently, we will have one hour of gunnery practice with live fire every morning before breakfast, after breakfast two hours of sailing evolutions. After lunch the men will do another hour of sail evolutions followed by aimed gunnery practice. I will be aboard the Hind moving up and down the line to observe."

**

The Hind became his flagship during daylight hours and speeded up and down the line as the evolutions were practised. Sail changes, top mast lowering and raising under sail, rapid changes of direction in formation. Changing from line astern to line abreast was a particular challenge with several near misses.

The Hind collected all the empty meat casks from the other ships and deployed them as targets. Marty wanted aimed fire at two cables to have a grouping within a ten-foot radius of the target. When a ship repeatedly failed or showed no improvement he went aboard and showed them it could be done by assuming the role of Gun Captain.

Then he watched each gun captain in turn and gave them pointers to improve their aim.

They were approaching Malta by the time he was happy enough with the sailing to practice formation changes again. All the captains managed to avoid coming up on a charge of negligence, just.

**

In Malta, Marty paid his respects to the governor. Major General, Sir Frederick Cavendish Ponsonby was, like Wellington, Anglo Irish. He had served at Waterloo in command of the Light Dragoons and almost suffered the same fate as the heavy cavalry who famously got carried away, went too far and were massacred by French Lancers. He was wounded seven times and only rescued after lying in the field for hours until found by a soldier of the 40th Foot who guarded him for several more hours until a cart picked him up and took him to the hospital.

Marty walked into the governor's office to be met by Ponsonby who walked with a decided limp. However, his handshake was firm and his eyes steady as he shook Marty's hand.

"Congratulations on your command, you have a fine fleet."

Marty thanked him. "Not enough on its own to defeat the Ottomans and Egyptians, but with the Russians and French we should be able to give them a hiding."

"There is a Greek representative here. Says he knows you. Bishop Germanos."

"I had the pleasure of meeting his eminence the last time I was out here. Where is he staying?"

"We are entertaining him here in the residence, I believe he is at Our Lady of Damascus, the Greek Orthodox Church here on the island holding a service at the moment."

He bade Marty to take a seat and poured tea.

"Milk and sugar?"

"Just a splash of milk please. What time does the service finish?"

Ponsonby checked his watch.

"In about half an hour. He will be back here at around twelve. Why don't we all have lunch together?"

Marty agreed as that gave him plenty of time to discuss things with the governor. He remembered his meetings with the bishop.

"You know Germanos is more than a priest?"

"Yes, he is somewhat of a diplomat and politically active as well. A very clever man."

"He is a senior member of the Feliki Etera and as such part of the government in waiting."

Ponsonby raised his eyebrows.

"Aah, that I didn't know. So, the new government will be secular?"

"No, not that I am aware of. A secular government would give the Russians far too good a reason to try and gather Greece in under its wing, and while the Greeks would prefer that to the Ottomans, we do not."

Ponsonby pondered that.

"Yes, I see. We want them as a self-governing state as part of the Ottoman Empire."

Marty nodded; his cup poised near his lips.

"That or truly independent, and we certainly do not want the Egyptians to march in and make Greece a Muslim state. My orders are to prevent the Imperial Squadron from annexing any of the Greek mainland or islands."

Ponsonby looked troubled.

"You will fire on them?"

"I will sink every last one of them if I have to, but we hope it will not come to that. If a blockade will stop them, that will suffice."

"Thomas Cochran and Hastings are in command of the Greek Navy?"

"That's putting it a bit strongly. They are advisors."

Ponsonby snorted a laugh.

"Call them what you like, my information is they are running it like a private navy."

That would be just like Thomas.

Just then there was a knock on the door and an assistant opened it to let Bishop Germanos in. The priest wore his usual black habit and hood with a golden cross resting just below his beard which had acquired some salt and pepper hints since the last time Marty saw him.

"Martin! I am so pleased to hear that you have command of the British fleet. Congratulations, will you accept my blessing?"

Marty stood, bowed and kissed the bishop's ring. Germanos placed his hand on his head and spoke in Greek. Once he finished Marty rose and the two took their seats.

"Are you here for any particular reason?" Marty asked.

"I came because we were informed of the accord between Britain, Russia and the French. It must have been a clever diplomat who persuaded the French to join. They have always been on the side of the Ottomans."

Marty cocked his head to one side.

"No diplomat, the French people were responsible. You see, the French government was working at odds to the will of the proletariat who generally admire the Greeks for wanting to be independent. Recent history has taught the king and government not to ignore the people as they are likely to rise up and bite them."

Germanos chuckled.

"The guillotine bites deep."

"And the terror is still fresh in their minds," Ponsonby added.

Marty asked the question that was forefront in his mind.

"Excellency, where do you think they will gather their fleet?"

"I have no doubt it will be Navarino. They have control of the town and the two forts. It is a safe haven for them."

Marty grinned wolfishly.

"And a perfect place for us to blockade if we must."

Germanos reached into his robe and took out a crucifix. It was silver with the extra short bar at the top and a diagonal bar where the feet of the golden depiction of Christ were nailed to it. There was a short inscription in Cyrillic on the back.

"This will identify you to any Greek as an ally, keep it with my blessing."

**

Marty used Malta as a base for the next two weeks to exercise his ships and hone their skills. Malta had ample supplies of powder and shot and a supply of old boats that could be used as targets. The captains were driven, and they drove their crews.

Marty introduced a competitive element by creating league tables by gun calibre. That way all the gunners on similar guns competed on speed and accuracy. The ship with the highest aggregate score of its rating was declared the winner and no ship was disadvantaged.

Second and third rates were in one league and as the Albion only had seventy-four guns, only the best seventy-four guns of the Asia and Genoa were counted. Similarly, the fifth rates competed as did the brig sloops and cutters all having ten guns. That left the Talbot and the Rose with twenty-eight and eighteen guns respectively.

To make things fair, each ship was monitored by a Shadow who took the timings and judged the accuracy. Marty was pleased with the outcome and called an all-captains' meeting.

"Gentlemen, do you all have a full glass?"

A chorus of "Aye, Sir."

We have the results, but first I want to congratulate you all for the improvements you have made. We are now ready to sail to Greece. Marty raised his glass. "To the Fleet."

"The Fleet!"

They drained their glasses to heel taps. Adam and the stewards refilled them.

"The best of the second and third rates was… the Genoa by one point, the narrowest of margins."

Bathurst was congratulated with slaps on the back.

"All three ships were within a point of each other. Next we have the fifth rates and the best ship there was… the Cambrian."

Marty waited until the congratulations had died down.

"Hamilton, your ship won by five clear points."

Marty cast an eye over the other three captains.

"You did well but you can learn something from Hamilton and his crew."

There was a round of teasing and banter.

"Now the ten-gun ships. The winner of those was… the Brisk. Another close-run race with only a point in it."

Marty turned to his son, James, and Davies of the Rose. He looked at the paper and raised his eyebrows.

"The Talbot and Rose both score exactly ninety-eight points each. It was a draw."

The two young captains grinned at each other and shook hands. Marty banged his glass for attention.

"There were three ships that scored ninety-eight points, which was the highest score. The Genoa, Talbot and Rose. I will give you all copies of the score sheet after dinner."

Diplomacy

Away from the fleet, diplomats were working hard to persuade the Ottomans to accept the Treaty of London which had been signed on the 6th of July. Marty was waiting for news as to the outcome, but until he heard otherwise, he assumed his ships would be needed. If the Ottomans refused, he would be transporting a consul to Nafplio, the Greek capital, to legitimise the Greek government. The consul was already on his way to Malta on the fast packet.

Marty decided to try some diplomacy of his own and sailed to Alexandria to see the assembling fleet for himself. His approach was noted well before they got to the harbour and a double-decked frigate came out to meet them. Marty decided to be cautious.

"Heave to. Have the men stand by their guns out of sight."

The Ottoman ship stopped within a cable and a boat was sent across. An officer bedecked in gold braid and with, Marty would describe it later as, a bouquet of ostrich feathers in his hat.

"Man the side for a captain," Marty said and Baines the first lieutenant barked the orders.

The bouquet appeared over the side with a face below it.

"Permission to come aboard?" it said in an Oxbridge accent.

"Permission granted," Curzon replied.

The officer stepped up onto the deck, adjusted his sleeves then addressed the waiting Curzon.

"I am Flag Captain Achmed Pasha, representative of Admiral Tahir Pasha."

Curzon introduced himself and asked, "How may I help you?"

"Very kind of you, old chap, but I see you are flying an admiral's pendant. I wish to speak with him."

"He is in his quarters; can I tell him what it's about?"

Achmed Pasha's face hardened, and he looked Curzon right in the eye.

"No, I will speak to him and only him."

Marty had expected this and had left instructions. Basically, keep it polite and friendly.

"Certainly, old chap, come with me and I will introduce you."

Curzon led Achmed Pasha down to Marty's day room. The marine knocked on the door opened it a crack and said, "The captain, Sir, with a foreign officer."

Curzon kept a straight face as he saw the look on the flag captain's face at being referred to as a 'foreign officer'.

The door opened, and they were ushered through.

**

Achmed took in the cabin at a glance. Typically British, a large desk made of some dark hardwood, probably mahogany, a chest of drawers with a three decanter tantalus and glasses surmounted by a portrait of a beautiful woman with auburn hair, a trio of comfortable leather club chairs that one would find in any gentlemen's club in London. The chairs were set around a rather nice occasional table. What jarred his eye was the large iron-bound chest, lying beside the chest of drawers below a wall mounted rack of swords and rifles. In front of that lay a very large brindled dog.

The admiral had risen from his chair and walked around the desk to meet him. The captain introduced them.

"May I present Admiral, Lord Stockley, Viscount of Purbeck. Admiral this is Flag Captain Achmed Pasha."

"Very pleased to meet you," the admiral said. He wore many honours on a scarlet sash including, Achmed noted, The Order of The Bath, Waterloo medal, Nile medal, Ottoman order of the Crescent and something that looked Indian, a gold tiger with blazing red ruby eyes.

"I bring greetings from my admiral Tahir Pasha." He went on to regurgitate all the honours the admiral bore.

Admiral Stockley waited patiently for him to stop and then invited him to sit and asked if he would like tea.

"Most kind of you." Achmed wasn't sure if he was talking to him or the servant who was serving the tea. "I was hoping to meet the admiral."

"You can, I have come to escort you to him."

"I presume that means you will not allow my ship to enter the harbour?"

"No, we will not. It is not permitted to get any closer than where it is right now, but you can come aboard my ship and I will take you to him."

"That could be possible if my flag lieutenant and coxswain accompany me."

The flag lieutenant had entered in the meantime and taken the third chair. He noted the captain had slipped away.

"Certainly, Sir. We rather expected you to ask for a larger escort."

The admiral smiled.

They finished their tea and the two British officers escorted him back up onto the main deck. His boat was waiting at the side and stood by the port was the largest African he had ever seen dressed in a blue jacket and white trousers. The admiral's smile broadened.

"This is Sam, my coxswain. Shall we go?"

The cox swung down the battens, agile despite his size, he was followed by the flag lieutenant. Achmed was next and the admiral last. The boat crew was overawed by the cox and their departure was ragged, much to the amusement of the British sailors watching from above. The large dog barked from where he stood with his front feet on the rail.

**

Marty and his men were confined to the captain's cabin so could only see the fleet through the transom windows. He estimated the ship, even though it was called a frigate, had sixty guns and could almost qualify as a third rate. Jeremy peered out after cleaning the glass with his handkerchief.

"There are a lot of Corvette-sized ships and more of these double-decked frigates. Some are quite scruffy."

The door opened and Achmed entered, he smiled as he saw what Jeremy was doing.

"We have a lot of ships, far more than the British Fleet."

"So, I see," Jeremy said, "are those fire ships?"

Achmed didn't answer.

"We will be alongside the Ghiuh Rewan directly, would you like to come up on deck?"

The Ghiuh Rewan was a third rate, eighty-four and was resplendent with gold paint and leaf around her stern.

"A pretty ship, boss." Sam looked across her deck.

Marty knew he did not mean that as a compliment even though Achmed beamed at it. The ship was spotless, all the brass and metalwork polished until it gleamed brightly in the sun. Leather fire buckets were polished to a shine and every rope was pristine. The crew looked smart but something about them jarred with Marty's senses.

An officer, Marty assumed was the captain, greeted them and Achmed translated.

"Welcome to my ship, the admiral awaits below."

They were taken below, and Marty noted there was no guard on the admiral's quarters. Achmed did not knock before leading them into the day cabin.

The admiral was sitting on cushions with a bowl of fruit on a low table beside him. As there were no chairs and he made no attempt to rise, Marty didn't bat an eyelid and joined him. Achmed bowed deeply. Sam stayed standing behind Marty and Jeremy sat awkwardly next to him.

The admiral cast an almost sneering look over them.

"What does the commander of the British Fleet want?"

That was deliberately rude, no formal greeting and no refreshments. He is trying to provoke me. Marty ignored it and replied calmly as if this happened every day.

"What I want is to avoid a conflict."

"Then leave the eastern Mediterranean and let us fight our own war."

"That is not possible, the Treaty of London is already in place. If your government does not agree to it the Russians, French and British will intervene and recognise Greece as a sovereign state."

The sneer became more pronounced.

"Even combined, your fleet does not match mine."

Marty decided to call his bluff.

"We out gun you and you know it. Your ships are the castoffs of the Europeans after the war and are manned by conscripts. Ours are manned by professional sailors who are well trained. Your officers have little or no experience in war and your French advisors will be recalled. Ours are all battle hardened. That is a fair assessment."

A flicker of uncertainty in the admirals eye told him he had hit the mark. Marty continued.

"Intervention is inevitable, the British want to have Greece as a self-governing nation as part of the Ottoman Empire which is what the Treaty proposes. Keep your fleet here and stay away from Greece."

The admiral kept a straight face, he had heard the same from the French the day before. Now he would ask his superiors if they wanted to change his orders. He sensed steel in the man before him who had the big (Nubian?) servant behind him.

"You are very blunt, Admiral Stockley," he said in English.

Marty kept his gaze steady and didn't react.

"Your reputation precedes you, and I know about your previous interactions with my sultan when you gifted him some traitors. Your affinity for the Greeks is also well known. I will consult with my superiors."

Marty nodded and stood, bowed in the Ottoman way as to an equal. The admiral rose and returned the bow.

"May God bless you and your family as he will our fleet."

Marty smiled ironically.

"I fear God will have little to do with this, and that hot iron and cold steel will decide the outcome."

**

Back on the Asia, Marty ate a cold lunch with his flag officers.

"Sam said he saw another third rate, at least half a dozen of their double-decked frigates, and a lot of corvettes. They also have fire ships."

Edward Curzon nodded over his plate.

"I wondered why you took him."

"He has sharp eyes, and the Turks look down on Africans as slaves so ignore them."

Curzon looked thoughtful.

"They have a lot of guns. Many more than we have."

"Aah but we fire faster and straighter, and our guns are bigger," Jeremy said.

It was Marty's turn to nod.

"Exactly, which is why I have spent so much time honing our crews."

"Do you think the French and Russians will be as good?" Edward asked.

Marty put down his knife and fork and patted his lips with his napkin. He was very serious when he relied.

"The French Levant Division will have crews that have probably seen a real fight before. The Russians have allocated half the Baltic fleet to this endeavour and their commander is experienced. They will arrive in Sicily sometime in September.

If we have to fight, we will be at the vanguard and face the bulk of the Ottoman fleet. I would rather fight with men I trust."

**

The Asia returned to Malta where Marty dispatched the Talbot to watch Alexandria with instructions to return with all speed if the Ottoman fleet left port. A note arrived from the governor requesting him to attend a meeting. Marty frowned when he read it as it was vague and did not tell him what the 'meeting' was about.

It was the tenth of July and hot. There was not a cloud in the sky and the sun was like a hammer.

Marty picked up his uniform bicorn hat,

"One with a broad brim would be more suitable," he sighed.

"Maybe this could help." Adam handed him an umbrella.

"That is an excellent idea. Thank you."

Marty left the ship by boat and as it crossed the water to the dock raised the umbrella for shade. Antton looked at and couldn't hide a grin.

"Don't mock," Marty said. "You don't have to wear a uniform and this hat."

It was true, Antton was dressed in a loose cotton shirt and trousers with a broad-brimmed planter's hat as were the rest of the Shadows. They would provide a discreet escort for him. Marty, as ever, was armed with two pistols concealed by the cunning cut of his coat, his fighting knife that was sheathed at an angle on the back of his belt to facilitate a left-handed draw, and his 1805 pattern sword was on his left. They reached the dock and Marty assessed the steps as the Shadows swarmed up them and spread out, the bottom three were green with algae.

He folded his umbrella and used it as a cane to steady himself as he climbed the steps. It absolutely wouldn't do to arrive at the governor's residence soaking wet. Sam had also spotted the danger and positioned himself to lend a hand if needed. Marty, however, made it up without incident and opened his umbrella before walking down the dock.

**

The residence was cool. He left his umbrella in a stand in the hallway and removed his hat to allow the sweat in his hair to dry. The clerk recognised him and escorted him straight to the governor's office.

Ponsonby rose from one of the comfortable chairs to greet him.

"Lord Martin, thank you for coming so quickly."

"Your note was vague enough to intrigue me," Marty replied.

A second figure rose from another chair.

"Hello, Frances." Marty smiled without turning his head.

Frances Ridgley laughed delightedly.

"How did you know it was me?"

I caught a glimpse of your cuff, and there is a faint smell of cardamom. You are still drinking chai I take it."

Frances' cuff was worn from the hours he spent going through reports from his agents.

"I will have to take care of that. I need a new suit anyway as they have made me consul in Greece."

Marty humphed.

"What better than to send a spy to do a diplomat's job."

They all sat down.

"Not much diplomacy needed, and Wellington thinks having someone on the ground in the thick of it would be… useful."

"Do you know if the Ottomans have agreed to it?" Ponsonby asked.

"I don't know if the allies have yet."

"Well, all we can do now is wait." Marty sighed.

Waiting & Watching

Marty kept the ships working in between shore leaves. The men might have to fight for their lives in the near future, so he wanted them both fit and rested. He took to playing brag with Frances who moved onto the ship. His latest orders were to wait and watch; wait for the Greeks to agree to the armistice and watch the Ottomans to see what they did.

Word arrived that the allies had signed the Treaty of London on the sixth of July, and that the Ottomans were under pressure to agree to its terms. The Greeks were waiting to see what the Ottomans would do.

Marty sighed as he read the message, which had been dispatched by fast packet. The news was already two weeks old. Frances was sat on the transom bench and took the message from Marty.

"Well, that's the first step. No new orders?"

"Nothing. I have letters from Caroline and the twins, but nothing from Dundas or Turner."

Frances looked a little chagrined.

"I should have told you, our local man has identified Ottoman and Egyptian spies on the island."

Marty perked up.

"Really? What should we do with them?"

"I suggest we get a capable agent here who can feed them false information."

"What's wrong with the one you have here?"

Frances shrugged.

"A good investigative agent but no good in the field."

"Hmm, who do you suggest?"

Frances got a sly look which Marty rightly interpreted as knowing something he didn't.

"They are sending reinforcements to Malta in case this turns into a land intervention."

Marty had an idea what was coming next, but he would let Frances have his moment.

"Which regiments?"

"The Welsh Guards and the 1st Battalion of the 95th."

"Sebastian's brigade," Marty stated.

Frances smirked.

"I have suggested that Beth come with him."

"Suggested?"

"Yes, I sent a note to Turner and Wellington on the packet two weeks ago."

"You have known that long?"

"As soon as I arrived."

Marty shook his head then looked up suddenly.

"The fleet should be at sea when she arrives. I need to send a message to London and to James on the Talbot."

**

The Fleet sailed and headed west at a fairly leisurely pace. Training exercises continued but not at the intensity of before. Marty went over every chart he had that covered the Peloponnese Peninsula and decided to head to the Ionian Islands. While they were there he wanted to talk to the British Agent in residence, Songbird.

They anchored on the British run Island of Zakynthos and found the Eagle and Endellion in port. He called their captains to him. Phillip Trenchard and Trevor Archer came aboard and were greeted by Jeremy.

"The admiral will see you in his quarters, this way, gentlemen."

Now neither of the two had any idea that Marty was the new commander in chief Mediterranean and had their commissions and letters of authority in their pockets just in case the admiral was going to try and recruit them.

The marine sentry announced them in a conversational tone of voice. Trevor looked at Phillip and raised his eyebrows. Then a familiar voice said, "Come."

They stepped inside.

"Good afternoon, gentlemen. I trust I find you well?" Marty said from behind his desk.

"All the better for seeing you, boss!" Trevor said.

"Not your boss this mission, they gave me the Fleet."

"CinC Mediterranean?" Phillip said, eyes wide in surprise.

Marty nodded.

"Congratulations!" they said in unison and laughed.

Marty got down to business.

"I want one of you to go to Valletta with messages and the other to take messages to Wolfgang and Cochrane."

Trevor raised his hand. "I am going to Valletta with a message from Songbird to her agent there."

Marty handed him three packets.

"One is for Beth who is or should be on the island by now. She is working undercover there as herself. She has two ships at her disposal, one is a schooner called the Fox and the other a cutter called the Cub. Keep an eye out for them on your way as she might try and find me for instructions."

 The second is for the port supplies officer and is a list of supplies I want ready to pick up in two weeks' time. The third is a report to be sent to London on the first available packet. Marty picked up another pair of packets.

"These are for Woldgang and Cochrane." He handed them to Philip.

"Now will you join me for a coffee?"

**

Veronica watched the fleet come in and saw the two captains' row over to the flagship. What she didn't see was the gig that left the flagship and landed Frances onshore. He made his way to her house on the plaza and knocked on the door. Billy answered it.

"The Kanis...... Mr Ridgley! What are you doing here?"

"Why, I'm visiting old friends. Can I come in?"

Billy was a big man, he swung the door open and when Frances stepped up swept him up in a bearhug.

"Got to make it look good," he muttered.

Once the door was shut, they proceeded in a much less demonstrative way up the stairs to what Billy called *the Songbirds Nest*. The door to it was open and Frances noted there were no visible handles or locks.

Inside was a room that sounded dull, so he assumed it was soundproof. It was lit by a skylight that had a blackout shutter that could be placed over it. Maps covered the walls with pins of various colours and little numbered flags stuck in them. A rack of weapons stood in a corner and an interesting chair that was obviously not meant for sitting on was in the opposite one.

Veronica, Songbird, was working at her desk and didn't look up when they entered.

"Let me finish this and I'll be right with you, Billy."

She kept writing and then sat back to sweep her hair out of her face.

"Frances! Where did you come from?"

"The flagship." He stepped forward and hugged his former student.

When he explained his role, Veronica looked perplexed.

"If you are looking for the Greeks to obey any kind of armistice with Cochrane and Hastings in charge of the Greek Navy, then you had better get your assassin's tools ready. Those two are bloodthirsty adventurers."

"Oh, I wouldn't worry about that. The chances of the Ottomans agreeing to the Treaty is little to none. The important thing is the Greeks do. Then Lord Martin can use his might to persuade them otherwise."

Veronica looked at him sharply,

"Lord Martin? M?"

"The very same, here as Commander in Chief Mediterranean."

Nothing else would do but for them all to go to the flagship.

**

Marty was delighted to see Veronica and Billy.

"It's good that you are both here because with Frances in the capitol you two can move back to Malta after this whole mess is settled."

Veronica was very happy at the news; she could resume her cover as an opera singer and Billy was just happy to be where she was. Marty wasn't finished.

"Frances will stay here so that as soon as we hear that the Greeks have agreed to the armistice, he can move to Nafplio with all dispatch. His presence will legitimise our intervention. In the meantime, I want you to compile a detailed record of Egyptian and Ottoman atrocities."

"How long do you think it will take?" Billy asked.

"For as long as it takes Lord Martin to destroy the Ottoman fleet," Frances said with a grin. Marty was not sure if he was joking or not.

Frances got serious.

"Look, as long as their fleet is shackled, they cannot reinforce their garrisons. That will allow the Greeks to roll them back. It will get to a point where it is costing too much in men to hold on to the territory they have already taken, and they will want to negotiate a peace."

Veronica interjected.

"But the Greeks are outnumbered, how can they win?"

Frances grinned.

"That is where the Ottomans scorched earth policy works against them. If we cut off their supplies by sea their troops will soon run out of food and..."

"An army runs on its stomach!" Billy cried.

"Exactly," Marty concluded.

**

Marty stayed in port for a week, estimating that Beth should have received the message and acted upon it, then sailed for Malta. It was deceptively calm and, if he didn't know better, the world felt at peace.

They might need to stay at sea for a protracted period so the shopping list that the Eagle had delivered was for six months of stores and enough powder to fill their magazines. Extra shot was needed to replace that used for practice. Luckily Marty's orders effectively gave him a blank cheque and he didn't have to dig into his personal finances at all.

Part of his strategy was to encourage the Ottomans to move their fleet to Navarino where he could bottle them up. So, he had asked Beth to spread the rumour that the Russian and French were at odds and that the French were unlikely to turn up. He also got her to leak that he was on his way back to Malta to reprovision. Having seen the Ottoman fleet in Alexandria he knew if they sailed, even with the time it would take the news to get to him, a fleet of that size would take several weeks to get there. He dispatched the Rose to replenish the Talbot and to act as messenger for James who he instructed to shadow the Ottomans if they left port.

**

They entered Valletta Harbour and fired a salute to the governor. Marty saw a group of figures stood on the wharf, raised his hat and waved. A large white dog sat with them.

He called Sam.

"Bring my barge around and have it manned. I am going ashore."

Hector immediately came and sat in front of him, looking up expectantly.

"I suppose you want to come with me. Well, it's about time you met Beth's dog." He put on Hector's town collar, which was leather, two inches wide and had a metal ring sewn into it. He attached a short chain leash to the ring, the other end of which was looped and bound in leather for a better grip.

The boat pulled up at the dock and Matai led Hector up the steps so Marty could ascend unimpeded. Beth's big Pyrenean was on alert but obeyed the command of its mistress to stay. Hector sat on command from Matai. The two eyed each other, ears erect, eyes bright wondering who was dominant. Marty had no intention of letting them find out.

"Matai, would you be so kind as to take Hector for a walk up to the park."

Beth looked relieved as Matai moved away. Hector wasn't so keen, he looked back and resisted. Fede took that as a threat and stood. Mike, one of Beth's team, stepped in and took the leash from her.

"I will take him so you two can talk."

He followed Matai from the dock but headed to a different park to exercise his charge.

"Those two will want a reckoning at some time," Marty said and hugged his daughter.

"Egyptian agent at four o'clock," Beth whispered.

Marty squeezed her hand in acknowledgement.

"It's wonderful to see you again, Father."

Marty knew that was for the agent's benefit, his daughter was playing.

"And you, how is that husband of yours?"

"Happy playing soldier; was your voyage pleasant?"

"Boring, I am not used to the inactivity imposed by being in command of a fleet. It's no wonder a lot of admirals get fat. The only thing I have to concern myself with is how I am going to make the French and Russians work together."

They started to walk, Beth's wolves in a group behind them with Sam. The agent picked up a box and walked in the same direction.

"The Ottoman's outnumber us," Marty continued, seemingly unaware that they could be overheard. "Without the French, well we have no hope of stopping them."

That was a double fallacy, he was totally confident he could beat the Ottomans on his own. They continued to chat like this until the agent was out of hearing.

"Is he the only one?" Marty asked.

"There is a Turk who runs a stand at the market. He has already been primed and sent a message. This one will send his tonight." Beth turned to her girls and made a signal. One kissed the other two and wandered off as if going into town. She would circle back to the docks and watch the agent.

"How is Mike working out?"

"Just fine. He gets on with the girls and respects them. He is very skilled and good with Fede."

"That dog is bigger than Hector now."

"Yes, and very protective. Do you think they would fight?"

"Probably but as soon as one proves he is dominant they would get on alright. If they were bitches, I would worry more."

"Why?"

"Because they tend to fight to the death." Marty grinned. "There's a reason they are called bitches."

**

As there was no news from James, Marty kept the Fleet in Valletta and waited. He was rewarded when on the eighth of August the Rose came into harbour flying the dispatches signal.

Marty called her captain aboard.

"What do you have to report, William?"

"The Ottoman fleet left port on the fifth. They took a day to form up, then anchored for the night. I left at dawn; the Talbot is shadowing them at a distance."

Marty pulled out a chart on which he had marked their potential route.

"With all those ships and inexperienced crews by the time they get them all under sail and into formation they will be lucky to make twenty-five miles a day. They dare not sail at night for fear of scattering the fleet."

"Gives us some time then, Sir."

"Indeed, it does."

**

Marty waited and was rewarded when the packet brought his final orders on the twentieth of August.

They instructed him to *"take all measures that circumstances may suggest to enforce the Allied demands if the Ottomans fail to comply within the specified time limit."* They also said, *"force should only be used as a last resort."*

Marty had complete freedom to act as he saw fit within those bounds, but he still needed to know whether they had signed or not!

Interlude

They waited. Marty found himself pacing up and down his cabin.

"This is no good. I need to get out," he said to himself.

"Sir?" Adam said as he poked his head through the door to the dining room.

"Get my barge manned, I'm going ashore."

"Yes, Sir."

"And tell them to rig a sling, Hector's coming with me."

"As you wish, Sir."

Marty growled something under his breath and Hector looked up from his sleeping mat.

"Come on, boy, let's go for a walk."

The big dog stretched then went to the door looking back over his shoulder as Marty put on a civilian coat and broad-brimmed hat after donning his fighting harness with two pistols.

The barge was waiting for him and the crew were ready with a sling to lower Hector over the side. He calmly stood as the specially made canvas was put around him and he was lifted up the out before being lowered to Sam who waited below.

Marty looked across at the shore and saw the ship's gig already halfway there. The Shadows were ahead of him. Hector safely aboard, Marty climbed down the battens, Sam was at the rudder with a midshipman beside him. Once Marty was seated, the mid gave the orders.

Once ashore he walked up the steps from the dock to the town above. It was, to all intents and purposes, a fortified town with walls, bastions and batteries protecting it. He had come ashore at Quarry Wharf and entered the town through the Liesse Gate. He wandered along with Hector at his knee in the general direction of the food market and found himself outside of the Church of St Paul of the shipwrecked. He paused to admire the façade which was ornamented with pillars and statues.

He was aware of someone approaching and Hector nudged his leg in warning. He turned and smiled as he recognised Mateus Falzon the Maltese chief of police.

"You have a new dog."

"I do. He is the son of Troy; his name is Hector."

Falzon laughed at the reference to the Odyssey.

They shook hands. Falzon scanned the street.

"I see your men are as watchful as ever."

"Yes, it's an ingrained habit. How is the policing business?"

Falzon smiled, he and Marty went back a long way and had several adventures together.

"Relatively peaceful, the consortium is behaving itself and we have only had two murders in the last year."

"Then you don't need my help."

Falzon shrugged. "I would only ask for that in the direst of circumstances."

"Let's get a coffee." Marty and the two made their way to a café.

It turned out to be just a social call and they chatted about family and mutual acquaintances. It did Marty the power of good and settled him more than anything else would.

There was a screech and a man bolted down the street followed by a woman who was screaming imprecations and waving a knife. Marty pointed and said, "Hector, fetch."

The two men sat relaxed as Hector tore off after the man and brought him down within fifty yards. Matai appeared and got him to release before dragging the man to his feet. Hector followed, ready to intercede if the man tried to run again.

The woman stopped screeching and reverted to giving the man a piece of her mind in Italian while waving the knife in his face. Matai took the knife from her and brought them both before Marty and Falzon.

Falzon asked the woman a question, to which she replied. He asked the man something and then turned to Marty, suppressing his mirth.

"He is her husband who she has just caught in the arms of another woman. He was running because she was going to kill him."

Marty chuckled. "A crime of passion then."

Falzon spoke sternly to the woman who paled and to the man who looked chagrined. He waved a hand at them, and they walked off. Matai gave the knife to the man then touched his forelock to Marty and wandered back to his post.

Falzon laughed. "That was rich. They are newly married. She is from Sicily and he was caught hugging another woman who turns out to be his cousin. She didn't wait to hear that and went for him with the knife. He ran to save his skin. I told her that she would hang here for killing her husband, our laws are different to Sicily."

Marty joined him in laughing at the comic situation.

"What did you tell him?"

"He said his family didn't approve of his marriage, so he hadn't introduced her. I suggested that it might be a good idea if he did."

Feeling refreshed, Marty returned to his ship. He and Mateus had spent the afternoon talking and Marty had confided in him the reason he was there. Mateus shone a perspective on it that helped Marty cope with the loneliness of command.

**

On the tenth of September the Talbot came into harbour under full sail. A superb display of seamanship saw her swing around and come alongside the Asia in a smooth arc. James came aboard and Marty met him at the entry port.

"The fleet has reached Navarino. We watched them enter, then headed back here to report. That was two days ago."

"Did you get a good count of their strength?"

"I did, it's all here in my report."

Marty patted his son on the shoulder.

"Replenish quickly, we will sail this evening. You can catch us up when you are ready."

Dismissed, James went back to his ship and moved her away to go alongside the wharf.

Marty looked to Captain Curzon.

"Raise the prepare, we sail in two hours."

This gave the ships time to recall any men ashore and soon guns were being fired as they signalled them to return.

The execute went up on time and sails blossomed. There would be stragglers who didn't get back in time, but James would gather them up and return them to their ships. He would forbid punishment unless a man deserted as two hours was not a lot of time if one was on the other side of the town.

**

Every ship was heavy with powder and ball. Marty was not worried about food as the Ionian Islands were close to Navarino and they could replenish from there. Under full sail they headed east, the men had an eagerness about them and practised their gun work diligently.

Marty still had not heard whether the Ottomans and Greeks had agreed to the accord, so he knew their arrival in Navarino would be largely symbolic. He wondered what was taking so long. However, he would make their presence felt and do what he could without starting a shooting war.

They arrived off Navarino Bay on the second of September and Anchored his liners outside the bay alongside the island of Sphacteria. His frigates kept up a constant patrol across the mouth of the bay.

Three days later, "Sail approaching from the north. Flying Greek colours and flying an admiral's pendant," a snotty nosed mid reported to Marty.

Marty pulled on his coat and hat, checked himself in the mirror and went up on deck as the frigate hove to a cable to windward. A boat was lowered and started across. Marty examined it through his small telescope.

"Captain, be so kind as to man the side for an admiral please," Marty grinned.

"Aye, aye, Sir."

Orders were bellowed and marines lined up, uniforms immaculate, pipe clay whitened belts gleaming in the sun. The ship's officers joined them, lined up in order of rank. Bosun's mates stood ready with their whistles in hand.

The boat pulled alongside and hooked on, moments later a hat appeared above the side. The marines crashed to attention sending up a cloud of pipe clay dust that blew away on the breeze. The bosuns whistles shrilled as the admiral of the Greek fleet stepped on deck and raised his hat to the quarterdeck.

"Permission to come aboard?"

"Granted. Hello, Thomas," Marty said, straight faced.

"Martin? Good God, man! An admiral no less!" Thomas Cochrane cried and shook the outstretched hand.

The two old friends restrained themselves for the sake of form and as the side party stood in the hot sun.

"May I introduce Flag Captain, Edward Curzon and Commander Robert Baynes, his first. Flag Lieutenant Jeremy Grandholm," they continued down the line. When they had completed the formalities, Marty led Thomas down to his quarters, Jeremy followed.

Hector looked up from where he had been dozing on his bed and saw someone new. He stood, stretched and wandered over.

"Still have a dog then," Thomas said as he ruffled Hector's head.

"That's Hector, Troy's son."

"He must have mated with a mastiff bitch then. Your shepherd was never this big."

"He did indeed. Please, sit. Adam, can you get us some coffee?"

The three of them sat. Marty and Thomas were relaxed and started to chat about the past.

"I wanted to attend your court martial, but the powers sent me away," Marty said.

"What happened to Gambier?"

"He commanded the Channel Fleet for a while, then was part of the delegation that negotiated the Treaty of Ghent in '14. I believe he got a Knight's Grand Cross and was knighted in '15. All due to his connections rather than exemplary service."

Jeremy got the impression neither man liked Gambier.

"Typical," Thomas huffed.

"He has been a thorn in my side, but my connections are as least as good as his." Marty grinned.

"The coward wouldn't want to take you on."

It turned out both men had been in South America at different times and Jeremy listened, fascinated, as the two recounted their adventures. Finally, they got around to the current situation.

"What are your orders?" Thomas asked.

"Simply to force the Ottomans into a ceasefire and armistice if they do not agree to the Treaty of London which allows Britain, Russia and

France to mediate self-government of Greece as part of the Ottoman Empire."

"What's to stop the Russians from stepping in and claiming Greece as part of their empire?"

"That's why the British came up with the Treaty. The last thing we want is the Russians expanding their empire. There are clauses in it that bind them to promise not to take any territory or commercial advantage from Turkey."

"What happens if they don't agree?"

"The Turks or Greeks?"

The Turks, I think, the Greeks will agree to it."

"Then I will enforce it."

Cochrane was serious when he said, "Be careful, Martin, the politicians never see things the way we do."

"I know, my orders have put the onus on me to decide what measures need to be taken. That way they can hang me out to dry if it all goes wrong."

"That is the way."

"It is indeed."

"I intend to try diplomacy first and try and to get their admiral to agree to a ceasefire."

Thomas was sceptical.

"Good luck with that. My orders are to continue as we have been."

"So, you will not stop raiding?"

"If the Greek government tells me to, of course I will. But my orders are to relieve the towns under siege and get food to the starving."

**

Marty decided he needed to know more about the situation on the land and dispatched the Shadows to inner Messinia to see how bad it really was. Antton led with Garai, Matai, and Chin. A four-man team was deemed enough for reconnaissance. Marty would have liked to have gone as well but the chains of seniority kept him on board.

The Rose dropped the team off down the coast at Methoni and they made their way inland. It was immediately obvious that the Egyptians and Turks had burnt crops and slaughtered all the animals. Any Greeks they met were starving and resorting to eating anything they could find. They travelled quietly avoiding Turkish patrols until they came across a heavily guarded supply convoy.

"That would feed an entire town," Chin commented as they looked down on the wagons that had settled down for the night.

"There are around thirty guards," Antton said.

"We have them beat." Garai grinned.

Matai was observing through a small pocket telescope.

"They are pretty confident, they only posted three guards."

Antton turned to Chin and held up a small bottle he took from his pouch.

"It will be dark in about half an hour. Do you think you can get the contents into that cauldron?" The soldiers were making a stew in a large cauldron and baking flatbreads on stones around the fire.

Chin grinned and took a set of folded black coveralls from his backpack.

**

Chin waited until it was properly dark and slipped down the hill, silent as a wraith, invisible against the dark ground. He easily bypassed the guards and crawled beneath the carts towards the central fire. The convoy guards were lazing around talking and smoking. He watched the cook who added something to the pot. The smell of spices, cinnamon and cumin, drifted towards him. He got within ten feet and stopped, there were too many soldiers in the way.

He backed up and made his way around to the cook's wagon. The man was rummaging around inside it. Chin waited. A foot appeared, then another, then a sack that was open at the top. He caught the scent of apricots. the feet turned away as someone said something to him. Chin's hand snaked out and emptied the bottle into the sack. He was very careful not to get any on his skin.

He immediately retreated to the darkness of the perimeter then slipped up onto the top of a wagon just in time to watch the cook empty the bag into the cauldron. He waited.

**

Up in the hill Antton watched and did not see Chin do anything. He saw the cook add things to the cauldron and stir it. He heard the soldiers calling out impatient for their meal. It was a half hour later when the cook was ready to serve them, and they lined up with their plates and mugs to get a portion of stew and a flatbread.

The guards were brought plates by their mates and soon the whole troop was tucking in. The meal finished, the soldiers cleaned and put away their plates to settle for the night. They waited for the ricin to take effect. The troops started to vomit, groans of agony started drifting up to them.

"Let's go," Antton said and the three slipped down the hill to the camp.

Chin had already been busy; they came across a guard who had his throat cut. Knives out, they moved through the camp dispatching any soldiers they came across. It was relatively easy work as the men were mostly disabled by the effects of the poison. They were all dead men walking anyway so killing them was a mercy.

One large trooper gave Matai a little more trouble and he had to actually fight him, but the result was the same. Soon the camp was quiet again.

"Check the wagons, we will only take the food," Antton said.

There were two wagons of powder and another two of shot. Antton took a brass object from his pack and climbed on top of one of the powder wagons. He broached one of the casks and set the dial on the top of the timer to three hours. He pushed the device down into the powder and replaced the lid. The timer was clockwork and had a spring-powered wheel that worked against a flint when the timer triggered. It had been developed and improved over the years by the incredibly talented men in the Toolshed. The SOFs useful things, research and development unit.

They harnessed up the horses to the food wagons and, lit by starlight, headed to the town of Finiki and left the wagons in the square. There were no soldiers in the town as the Turks were confident their policy had defeated the Greeks who wouldn't have the strength to fight.

The sun was just breaking the horizon when a huge column of smoke lit by an enormous column of flame rose to the west of the town. It was followed by the sound of a loud explosion which woke the inhabitants. Startled people came out of their houses and saw the wagons. The bravest approached and saw the tailgates were open and bags of flour and beans were arranged as if on display. The mayor prevented a riot and organised the contents to be distributed and hidden. The wagons were burnt, the horses taken out of town to hidden pastures in the hills. The Shadows went along the back trail and brushed out the cart tracks.

Agreement

A fast packet found the fleet on the seventeenth of September. Its commander, one lieutenant Williams, came aboard the Ganges with a sealed packet that Marty had to sign for. In it was a copy of the Treaty with the signatures of the Prime Minister of Britain, Russian Ambassador in London (on behalf of the Tsar Nicholas I). French Ambassador (on behalf of King Charles X) and Greek Ambassador (on behalf of the Greek government). There was no signature from the Ottomans. Also enclosed were letters from Arthur and Julia Turner. The one from Arthur read.

To Admiral Stockley

Martin
The Ottomans have formally rejected the Treaty of London. They think themselves too powerful to be threatened by a lesser force even if constituted of ships from all the allies. Step carefully and exhaust all diplomatic avenues before resorting to force. I say this because there is a significant group of members who are against any intervention on our part.

I do not think you will have heard but George Canning passed away on the 8th August of tuberculosis, may God rest his soul. Viscount Goderich, Frederick Robinson, has stepped in as Prime Minister and is not half the statesman that George was. He supports the intervention but has little influence. I believe I shall be asked to take the position come the new year.

Your daughter and son-in-law have been recalled to London. The situation in South America needs experienced agents on the ground and we have appointed Sebastian as Attaché to the Minister in Columbia with a roving brief.

As ever, your friend

Arthur

The letter from Julia Turner was more disturbing.

My dear Martin,

I write to you on behalf of James who is confined to bed with Cholera Morbus. I fear he contracted it from an agent that had been in India for some time. The disease is spreading across Europe like wildfire from Asia. The doctors do not have a clue how to treat it and just offer to bleed him.

He asked me to write this as a warning that in the case that he does not survive, you are his named successor and have the support of Arthur

Wellesley. God forbid it comes to that but if it does he says he has absolute faith that you will do your duty by him and the country.

I wish you fair winds and good fortune in your present task and all our love.

Julia

"Something wrong, Sir?" Adam asked.

"Admiral Turner is ill, I do not believe he thinks he will survive it."

"That is indeed bad news. Do they know what it is that ails him?"

"Asian Cholera. It has spread across Europe. I only hope that as he is fit, he may weather the storm."

Marty folded the letter and put it away. He sighed, the last job on this earth he wanted was to be trapped behind a desk as Head of the Foreign and Overseas Office. He shook himself; this would not do; he had a job to do.

He took a fresh sheet of paper and wrote a note to the admiral of the Ottoman fleet asking for a meeting. His goal was to avoid hostilities and try to come to some agreement with them that, despite their rejection of the Treaty, achieved roughly the same goal.

He also wrote a note to Frances telling him to proceed to Napfilion with all dispatch. He would loan him the Hind as the city was situated on the Gulf of Argolic in the northeast of the Peloponnese. This was probably the most defensible town in Greece as it was virtually cut off from the land by marshes and wetlands. As long as Marty kept the

Ottoman fleet bottled up, he would be safe there. Finally, he wrote a note to Veronica telling her to return to Malta where she would be better used misdirecting the Ottomans.

The letters to Veronica and Frances were handed to Midshipman Grant with orders to get Frances to Napfilion as soon as possible then return to the Fleet. The letter to the admiral was taken by Jeremy aboard the Asia's long boat into the harbour under a white flag of parlay. He returned with an agreement to meet after the admiral had received official notification from his government as to their stance on the matter.

**

A report arrived from Wolfgang, carried by Philip Trenchard on the Endellion, saying the Greeks were planning further attacks on the Turks and that they had acquired a steam-powered warship, the Kartèria, a sloop-of-war. She had been requisitioned by Captain Frank Hastings, a former Royal Navy officer, from a British shipyard and carried four big sixty-eight-pound carronades and four even bigger sixty-eight-pound cannon. Propulsion was a mixture of sails on four masts and paddlewheels which made her manoeuvrable and able to sail directly into the wind.

Hastings was the grandson of the 10th Earl of Huntingdon and had served at Trafalgar in the Neptune and at the Battle of New Orleans, but left the navy in 1819. He espoused the use of steam and direct fire with hot or exploding shot as the way forward for naval gunnery. Personally, Marty thought he would like the man as he was a visionary.

Wolfgang's report also warned that General Richard Church was intent on shifting the fight to the Gulf of Corinth. He had previously tried to liberate Athens but the Greek's inability to execute any form of regular operations due to their total resistance to following orders had led him to fight a partisan war in the west.

Not wanting to have the SOF mixed up in anything Hastings was about to do he sent a message back with Philip recalling the flotilla to Zante. Now all he could do was wait.

**

The Ottoman Navy was not as efficient in the transmission of signals as the British or maybe it was because all communications had to go through Constantinople, but it was not until the twenty-fifth that Marty was invited to visit the Ottoman flagship to meet Ibrahim Pasha and Admiral Amir Tahir. He was accompanied by Jonathan and Sam as before.

Marty made himself comfortable on the cushions and accepted a glass of mint tea. Ibrahim Oasha opened the discussion after the mandatory pleasantries.

"My government informs me that they have rejected the Treaty of London."

Marty nodded.

"So I have been informed. As a consequence, the allies have installed consuls in Nafplion the capital of Independent Greece and thereby recognised the Greek government as the legitimate government of Greece and Greece as a Sovereign Nation. My orders are to enforce the allies demands and to mediate a ceasefire."

"You are outnumbered, where are your allies?"

Marty had no idea but had faith that they would be on their way.

"They will be here soon."

He leaned forward.

"I want to avoid any more bloodshed. We can do that and let the governments sort the whole thing out between them. Let us agree to a ceasefire and save lives on both sides."

"Do you speak on behalf of the Greeks?"

"I will talk to them as well, but it would show good faith if you agreed in advance of that."

Ibrahim consulted with Amir Tahir. Marty didn't understand a word that was said but he thought the looks on their faces were a mixture of distrust and contempt. He was therefore surprised when Ibrahim turned back to him.

"We agree as long as the Greeks cease their attacks, we will cease ours."

Marty noted that he didn't mention lifting any sieges and so did Jonathan who whispered in his ear. Marty murmured back.

"I noticed; diplomacy is sometimes more about what is not said than what is."

Marty turned to Ibrahim.

"Can I get your promise that you will cease hostilities by land and sea?"

"We will agree to a ceasefire and promise to respect it as long as the Greeks do."

**

Marty ordered the Dartmouth to remain on station and ordered the rest of the fleet to Zante (Zakynthos). He took the Rose to Nafplion to talk to the Greek government who tentatively agreed with the same caveats as the Turks.

Marty met with Frances.

"I have agreements but no faith," Marty said.

"Your problem, my friend, is going to be Cochrane and Hastings. The Greek government has no control and little influence over them."

"I was afraid of that. Thomas is a hot head and prefers action to words."

"And Hastings is doing it in the belief of the Greek cause. He is not even taking pay."

"Lord protect us from those with a cause!" Marty said piously looking to the heavens.

**

In Zante James Stockley received mail, in it was a letter from his wife Melissa.

My dearest James

I miss you so much when you are away. Beloved I am well and definitely pregnant! Morning sickness is a bother, but Caroline assures me it will stop by the fourth or fifth month. I have a visible bump now and am overjoyed that I am carrying a new life inside of me.

James stopped reading and looked out of the transom window at the fleet anchored behind his ship. They had suspected that she may have fallen before he left. Beth had actually asked outright if Melissa was pregnant triggered by some kind of womanly instinct. He trusted her instincts which were as acute as their father's. Now he knew for sure she was and would have to tell his father he was going to be a grandfather.

He read on.

We have received bad news about James Turner. He has contracted Asian Cholera and, because I am pregnant, Caroline has refused to visit them in the fear she may bring the disease home with her. Julia is having to manage very much on her own but understands the situation. The latest report is that he has become very weak and frail.

James checked the date on the letter; it was the tenth, over two weeks old. Turner could be dead by now. He felt a great sadness, James was like an uncle to him. Then he had a thought; did that mean his father was now head of the Foreign Intelligence Service?

He read the rest of the letter which covered news about the twins and from the country in general. She had enclosed a copy of *The Times* which featured George Canning's funeral in Westminster Abbey. A lavish affair unprecedented for a Prime Minister and attended by thousands.

A gun sounded and he put the letters away into a drawer in his desk and locked it. He went up on deck to see the Rose come into port.

"Have my boat brought around and manned," he ordered.

**

There was a knock at the door and the sentry said, "Captain Stockley, Sir."

"Come."

His son walked with a smile on his face.

"James! This is an unexpected pleasure. Come sit. Coffee?"

"Yes please."

"Meriweather! Coffee for two if you please."

"No Adam?"

"Ashore with Rolland."

That explained it. The two would be shopping for a dinner.

"So, what brings you here?" Marty asked to the background hiss of the pressure cooker.

"I have had a letter from home."

Marty looked at his son's beaming face.

"Good news by your grin."

"You, my dear father, are going to be a grandfather."

Marty leapt to his feet and hauled his son upright to hug him. The door opened and an astonished Meriweather stood there holding a tray.

"You hear that, Meriweather? I am going to be a grandfather!" Marty crowed.

"Congratulations, Milords," he said, put the tray on the desk and moved over to the tantalus on the sideboard to pour two large brandies and place them on the small table between the men's chairs. He then discretely retired and rushed out to the gundeck to spread the news to his mates.

In the cabin things turned to a more serious matter.

"I heard about James Turner," James said.

"Yes, it is grave news. Julia wrote to me."

"It seems he is unlikely to survive, will you take over?"

"If Arthur asks me to, I will. Though I do not relish the task."

James looked at his father seriously. "According to the newspaper Melissa sent me, Robinson won't last beyond the new year and Arthur is expected to be appointed Prime Minister then. He will want someone he can trust in the position."

Marty sighed. Every silver cloud had a dark lining.

**

By the time James emerged the whole ship knew his good news, and a great cheer went up as he took to his boat. He stood and waved his hat in acknowledgement, laughing in joy.

Hastings

Despite Marty's plea for a ceasefire which had been verbally agreed by the Greek provisional government, Sir Richard Church, Thomas Cochrane and Frank Hastings, the British commanders of the Greek forces, were planning actions.

Church was planning to lay siege to Patras, Cochrane to start a rebellion in the province of Eprius and most importantly Hastings was planning an action against the Ottoman gunboats in Salona Bay. Between him and Church they were shifting the focus of the war against the Ottomans to western Greece closer to the British Fleet.

Hastings had commissioned his steam sloop Kartèria from an English shipyard in accordance with his views on the future of naval warfare. He firmly believed that aimed hot shot and shell would supplant the use of fire ships and was about to prove it. While Church laid siege to Patras he steamed his ship out of the port of Germeno on the 29th September.

Crewed by a mixture of English, Swedish and Greek men, she was unlike any other ship in the region. The magazine was full of exploding shot for the four sixty-eight-pound cannons. These were primed with four pounds of gunpowder and a fuse that was ignited by the flash of the propellant. The skill was in cutting the fuse to the right length so that it exploded just before or over the target. No other ships were using this type of shot at that time.

The four carronades were primarily employed to defend the ship and anything that got close enough to come into their arc of fire was doomed as they fired hot shot heated in an oven on the deck.

**

"It will be dark in an hour," George Knight, the first lieutenant, remarked as they left port at around six in the evening.

Hastings looked at his watch and listened for the log to be called.

"Eight knots, we should be entering Salona Bay at around midnight. We will open fire on the Ottoman squadron from a mile and a half out and close to a hundred yards."

"It will be warm work for the gunners."

"Each gun has three crews; they should be able to keep up a steady fire for several hours if need be."

"True but if you don't mind, I will allocate men to help with the shells. Them being so heavy and all."

Hastings nodded. He knew what Marty's orders were and wanted to provoke the Ottomans into trying to leave Navarino to either try and relieve Patras or chase him down. Either way Lord Stockley would have to respond, and it would take just one shot to set off a confrontation.

**

They sailed through dusk and into the night lit by a moon that was approaching full and gave enough light to sail by. Scudding clouds flew from west to east reflecting the prevailing wind. Hastings smiled; he was free from the wind. His steam paddles could drive the Kartèria along at eight knots wherever it blew from and now he was sailing as no canvas powered craft could. Directly into it.

He knew that the Ottomans thought they were safe from his tiny navy, but they didn't know about the Kartèria. She was not forced to tack endlessly to make headway west along the Gulf travelling twice as far as she needed to. They were also unprepared for exploding shells fired from a ship, or the manoeuvrability his paddles gave him. He didn't need to anchor and attach springs. He had invested seven thousand pounds of his own money into the Kartèria and she was going to be worth every penny.

The rhythm of the engine was almost hypnotic. The steady chuff from the funnel and the sound of the wheels pushing through the water. The feel of the engine vibrated through the deck like a heartbeat.

They took sightings from landmarks on the shore and islands pinpointing their position far more accurately than by dead reckoning. There was the Alkionides, that heralded their entry into the main body of the Gulf. Paralia Bay, the island of Saint Lucas, the church of Saint Pankalos on its headland and then they were in the bay and able to turn north. The slowed to four knots and closed quietly up on Itea. The men came to quarters. The first two fuses were cut to explode at two thousand six hundred and forty yards. Hastings knew the small rocky outcrop called Galaxidi was just under one and a half miles from the harbour. He slowed the ship to just three knots, and swung the bow to bring his starboard guns to bear.

The gunners squinted along the barrels, there was no need to aim precisely, the harbour was full of ships. The gunners raised an arm to indicate readiness.

"Fire!"

One could just pick up the glow of the fuse as they flew towards the harbour and the squadron of ships/gunboats moored there.

The shells exploded in the air as the gunners were busy reloading. He swung the bow to port to bring the other two guns to bear. zig-zagging towards the port they fired two exploding shells every minute.

**

In the town the citizens were rudely awakened by the thunder of the shells exploding. The Ottoman sailors found their world turn into a hell of screaming metal shards and fire.

What is happening? What the hell was that? Are we under attack? Were questions asked by officers and men alike. Confusion reigned; men ran to their guns but didn't have anything to shoot at. Then the second shots were heard, and someone saw the muzzle flashes.

"Over there!"

Any orders were drowned out by the two massive explosions above their heads. A ship caught fire.

"Cut the mooring lines, man the oars!"

Men scrambled to their posts the sound of axes cutting cables echoed.

KABOOM! a shell exploded directly above a galley shattering it into firewood and killing almost all the crew. Another burst closer to the shore sending shrapnel hissing into the sea.

**

As they crept closer and ships started to burn, illuminating the harbour, they were able to aim more accurately. Small adjustments in heading, aided the gunners and as they closed, the carronades joined in. Every ten rounds the gunners were changed, the barrels got hot and had to be quenched. Steam and smoke drifted away across the water blown by the westerly night breeze.

Targeted fire now came into play as the silhouettes of ships could be clearly seen against the flames. They were firing at effectively point-blank range and the Ottomans didn't stand a chance. Shell after shell exploded above, in and alongside the squadron.

As the sun rose, a scene of devastation was revealed. The harbour was littered with wreckage and the shoreline was battered and scorched. Several warehouses were burning, as were a couple of houses. Hastings was not satisfied. He ordered the helm to steer into Itea Bay and looked for any boats that may have escaped. He found them, when two attacked from Larnakia.

"Ready the carronades with small ball."

The gunboats were trying to get as close as possible before they fired their twenty-four pounders and waited until they were at four hundred yards before firing. The Kartèria fired at the same range sending a wall of four pound shot hurtling across the water.

Hastings watched as the gunboats shuddered as they were torn apart. Their shots passed over his deck and caused a little damage to some rigging.

Turning around they steamed back to Itea and surveyed their work. Nine ships had been destroyed including the two in the bay. Locals said that two more had escaped.

They turned for home raising the sails to make use of the wind that was now on their stern. The first steamship action in history was over.

Repercussions

Bad news travels fast, is the old adage, and it certainly did in this case. The day after Hastings attacked Itea, Marty was asked to meet Ibrahim Pasha and Admiral Amir Tahir.

He entered the admiral's cabin and felt the anger in the room immediately.

"Why do you not control the Greeks?" Amir Tahir shot at him.

Marty sighed. "What has happened?"

"They have attacked our fleet at Itea and sunk nine ships!"

Marty had an inkling as to who was responsible.

"What ship did this?"

"The report says one that used no sails to move and fired exploding shells."

"Hastings. A former British officer, along with Church and Cochrane, are commanding large parts of the Greek army and navy. Hastings has a steam-powered warship. Unfortunately, they act largely on their own initiative."

"You are saying the British did this?"

"No, I am saying that the officers in command work for the Greek Provisional Government but operate largely independently."

"You must stop them, or the agreement will be broken."

"I will send envoys to them and demand they stop. Give me the time to do that." Even as he said it he could see in their eyes the frustration and anger. "I should be able to reach Church today, Cochrane and Hastings are further away."

They said nothing and Marty bowed his way out.

**

On his return Marty immediately sent three midshipmen to find the British commanders. He had absolutely no confidence that they would have any influence at all and strongly suspected the Ottomans were out of patience.

"Prepare the fleet to sail. All shore leave is cancelled immediately," he ordered.

Two guns were fired indicating the command was an imperative and soon boats were bringing back sailors from a crowded wharf. By midday they were ready to sail. Marty paced, and hoped the Dartmouth could stop any attempt by the Ottomans to send aid to Patras which, being besieged from the land, could be reinforced from the sea.

Marty sent the Talbot, Glasgow and Cambrian out to reinforce the Dartmouth. Independently they could make eleven to twelve knots and get there before dark even having to make long tacks against the southerly wind.

**

James was exhilarated, his ship was under full sail, she could not carry another handkerchief of canvas. Not only that she was holding her own with the two big frigates. To stay with them he was having to use all his seamanship and keep his sail handlers on their toes. A sail shivered, they were sailing as close to the wind as they could.

"Trim the main gallant!"

They were on the very edge.

"Eleven knots and a fathom," Midshipman Rogers called from the chains.

"She is flying!" Ed Pascoe, the first lieutenant, crowed.

The Talbot had a young set of officers. Ed was just twenty-six years old, the second twenty-four and James was just twenty-five. That meant they had enthusiasm in spades and were gnashing at the bit to get into a fight.

"She is indeed, Ed," James replied.

"If we wet the sails, we might get twelve out of her," Ed said.

James concentrated on the gap between them and the Glasgow. It was being maintained at the appropriate two cables.

"No need, we don't want to embarrass our seniors." James grinned.

Two hours later a signal went up from the Glasgow, *enemy sighted,* followed by, *line abreast.*

"Wet the sails!" James ordered.

The extra half a knot allowed them to get into position without having to ask the Glasgow to slow. James looked up at the sails then across the deck. The men were quietly getting ready to go to quarters. This was a good crew.

"Deck there, the Dartmouth is on the windward side of the enemy ships."

James jumped up on a carronade and put a telescope to his eye.

Ottoman Squadron, A seventy, a forty-eight, two Brigs and three corvettes.

"Signal from Glasgow, *quarters,*" Midshipman Rowe reported from somewhere near James's feet.

"Go to Quarters!" James bellowed and the ship became a hive of activity.

"Eight minutes," Ed announced, watch in hand.

"Open ports!" James ordered. He would let his betters know they were an efficient ship. It was noted on the Glasgow, Captain Maude commented to his first, "As keen as his father."

The signal, *run out,* came.

The carronades were loaded with smashers already and the deck shook as they were run out. A flurry of flags flew up on the Glasgow. Midshipman Rowe furiously translated the spelt-out part.

"*Prepare fore chasers.*"

"Load the nines. I think he wants to send a message."

"Aye, aye, Sir," Ed replied and ran forward.

The enemy was still a mile ahead when the *execute* command was given.

"Fire!" Ed barked and the guns spoke.

**

On the Ottoman third rate, her captain watched the black dots that got bigger as they approached. A row of splashes ahead of his ship showed the fall of shot. It was grouped nicely.

His instructions were clear. Avoid a direct confrontation with the British but get the supplies to Patras.

"They will not fight us; they just seek to intimidate. Maintain your course, the wind is in our favour.

**

Captain Maude watched the fall of shot and saw that the Ottomans did not flinch, nor did they run out in response. His orders were to only fire on them if fired upon. He had already stretched that to the limit.

"Damn, I hoped that would get them to turn back. Signal the Talbot to come within hail."

**

James brought the Talbot up to within hailing distance. Maude bellowed orders through a speaking trumpet.

"Go to the Fleet and tell them the Ottomans are seeking to reinforce Patras. We will shadow them."

James doffed his hat in acknowledgement and ordered, "Wear ship."

With the wind on their stern they sped away north heading directly for Zante. Even so they were only running three knots faster than the Ottomans. Would the fleet be able to respond in time?"

**

Marty was warned that the Talbot was approaching, flying a signal. It read, *Enemy in Sight.*

"Raise the preparatory, get us under sail."

Captain Curzon started issuing orders which echoed down the ship. Men tramped around the capstan and the anchor cable came in until the shout, "Anchor is up and down!"

Sails blossomed on the fore and mizzen and the execute signal flew. Another turn on the capstan and the anchor broke free.

"Catch her helm," the first called.

"We have steerage," the helmsman replied.

"Steer west," Marty ordered. "We will close the entrance to the Gulf."

His intention was to stop the Ottomans in the ten-mile-wide gap between Zante and the mainland before they could turn into the Gulf of Corinth. He also hoped they would turn back without starting a fight although he was quite prepared to if forced.

He watched the other ships respond. He had issued orders for just this occasion and the ships fell in around the Asia in the order he required. Asia, Genoa and Albion would be in the centre of the line with the sloops Brisk and Musquito ahead and the Talbot and Philomel behind. The cutter, Hind, would repeat signals on the windward side.

They entered the gap in line of battle and it was a scant hour before the mainmast lookout, who was as high up as he could get, called, "Sails to the south!"

Marty knew that had to be the Ottomans and that they were more than eighteen miles away with the wind on their stern. He estimated that even they could make eight knots in the prevailing conditions. Therefore, he could expect them to be up on them in a little over two hours. That gave him time to position his ships exactly where he wanted them.

**

On the Burj Zafer the captain watched the line of sails come up over the horizon. The frigates that had been shadowing them, dropped back to windward and formed a line astern of his squadron. He had the wind gauge on the fleet ahead which was presenting its broadside to him, but the heavily armed frigates had the wind gauge on him. He was caught in a trap.

Swearing profusely, he said, "Order the squadron to return to Navarino we can achieve nothing here."

**

Marty watched the Ottoman Squadron wear in line. It was untidy but they got the job done.

"Wear ship, we will escort them back to the bay."

His ships manoeuvred with absolute precision, each turning in exactly the same spot. Marty felt a glow of pride at the sight. As they passed Zante the fast packet was arriving and diverted to deliver mail to the flagship. This was done at eight knots with the ships sailing beside each other and the mail being hauled aboard on a lift line that was fired across from the flagship to the packet.

Marty sat in his cabin and opened the official letters first. They were mostly the usual dispatches asking for his reports and state of stores. Then one caught his eye. It was in Arthur's handwriting. Marty's heart sank as he opened it. It had no preamble and was written in black ink.

My dear friend

I have the misfortune to be the bearer of the saddest of news. Our mutual friend and colleague James Turner has succumbed to his illness and died on the 14th day of September. He will be buried at the Chapel of St Peter and St Paul at the Naval College in Greenwich on the 17th.

His wife and children are being cared for by the service led by your good lady wife.

I am reluctant to burden you further but, on your return, you are to take over the position as head of the Foreign and Overseas branch. I need someone I can trust there. You have also been promoted to Vice Admiral.

Marty let it fall from his fingers and hung his head. James Turner had been a presence in his life for all the time he had been at sea, and he counted him a dear friend, mentor and colleague. To lose him when he was only seventy-five years old...

True, the lifespan of the average male was around sixty-five years at the time, but navy officers were fitter, better fed and tended to live much longer. Hood had lived well into his eighties.

Tears ran down his face and he wept quietly for a while. Recovering himself and washing his face in the bowl by his bed, he returned to his day room and called Adam.

"Can you ask the Shadows to gather here in my cabin please. All of you, including Roland."

The men gathered. They had all known James at one time or another, some for as long as Marty had.

"I have grave news. Admiral James Turner has passed away. I wanted to tell you myself as you old hands all knew him from when we first met. He was a truly great captain and, as the head of the foreign branch, showed exemplary leadership, judgement and always had our best interests at heart. Even when sending us into dangerous situations."

That caused a wry chuckle.

"I will ask the ship's chaplain to hold a short memorial service as we have all missed his burial. Adam, would you please be so kind as to serve everyone a glass of port."

Once they all had a glass in front of them Marty stood in the centre of what was now a ring of men. He raised his glass and turned to look each man in the eye.

"To Admiral James Turner, a steadfast friend."

They drained their glasses after shouting "James Turner!"

Then Antton threw back his head and let fly with a Basque mountain salute to the dead. The eery cry, Ayee, Ayee, Ayee, yo, yea, Ayee! was taken up by the rest of them and seeped up to the quarterdeck.

"What the hell is that?" Captain Curzon said as the hairs on the back of his neck rose at the lament.

The memorial service was held at noon. The chaplain did not know James so Marty gave the eulogy.

"James Turner was the man who brought me into the navy. I was just twelve years old when he made me his cabin boy. He was the fighting captain of the Falcon, my first ship. Renowned for his zeal and his hunting horn which he would blow as soon as the hunt was on for a prize.

James became an admiral and head of the foreign branch of the Intelligence Service at the same time. Often referred to as a pirate by his peers because of the 'unofficial' nature of many of his doings he was politically astute and acutely aware of the hidden dangers presented by other nations and the need to counter them.

He was no saint but a good man who did what had to be done. He shall be missed and has set a standard that will be hard to match.

His wife Julia survives him. She was the love of his life found after an extensive search in many ports around the world. They had two wonderful children; their son is first lieutenant on the Boyne and is following in his father's footsteps.

God bless him and take him into his arms."

The service over, Marty turned to the job in hand. The future could wait.

**

A storm blew up on the third of October making the night as dark as the devil's soul. It was not a bad one but it gave Ibrahim the chance to sneak another squadron out past the British. Marty realised what they had done as soon as it got light and set out in pursuit leaving a pair of frigates behind to patrol the entrance to the bay.

The wind was against them, and they had to beat against it all the way up to the Gulf. Tack followed tack until the evening of the fourth.

"Deck there. Masts behind Cape Pappas!"

The wind had swung to be more from the east and was a rank muzzler preventing any ships entering the Gulf.

"They almost made it," Curzon commented.

"God must be on our side," Baynes replied.

They were well wrapped up in heavy coats against the wind and rain. Marty had the weather side of the deck snug in a tarpaulin coat and sou'wester hat. Curzon did not approve of such an informal mode of dress even though Marty was by far and away the most comfortable of the two.

"Move us up in line of battle," Marty ordered after studying the anchored ships. "Bring the fleet to quarters; we will get them moving with a thrust from our broadside."

"Loaded with shot?" Curzon asked.

"Chain over shot, we will fire high, over their masts."

The signal was complex, but the signal officer managed it and the ships soon had their starboard guns run out. Jeremy wondered where all the balls would land but Marty reassured him that behind the Ottoman ships was a lagoon where the shot would land safely.

The fleet fired in succession, each broadside howling above the squadron's masts. The combination of ball and chain created a sound unlike anything else, an eerie wail of a howl that raised hackles. Hector joined in to the officer's amusement.

The encouragement had the desired effect. Ibrahim ordered his ships to make sail and headed south back to Navarino. Marty had the fleet form an arc that curved around their stern up to the flagship and shepherded them along.

Slash and Burn

Ibrahim was not happy. He was in danger of losing Petras and the revolt in the northwest was gaining momentum, neither of which he could affect while he was trapped in Navarino Bay. He could, however, do something with the troops he already had on the peninsula.

"If we cannot advance the plan by sea we will do it by land," he told his generals.

The soldiers in his ships were put ashore and advanced through the countryside. Behind them they left the smoking ruins of crops and towns strewn with the bodies of farmers, labourers and merchants. Beef and goats, they drove along with them. Their supply wagons were always full. An army has to eat after all.

Joining up with the army already on the peninsula twenty-five thousand men turned north to relieve the siege of Petras. The five thousand Greek partisans were outnumbered and in danger of being trapped against the sea

Marty wanted to know what was going on and to warn Church to get away if needed. So, the Shadows went ashore again and set out to catch up with the Egyptian/Turkish army. They moved across the barren landscape at a fast march covering twenty-five miles a day. They carried rucksacks with all their food and ammunition that weighed in at almost fifty pounds to begin with.

What they saw was horrible. Wells were poisoned by having dead animals and people thrown into them. Rivers and streams likewise. They had real trouble finding palatable water. Then there were the survivors of the army's passing. Starving, stick-thin people, some barely alive.

Rotting corpses were everywhere and the risk of disease was high. Crows and wild dogs got fat on the abundance of carrion. Disease would follow, it was an inhuman way to make war.

Some villages had obviously tried to resist and the further north they went the more they saw evidence of open rebellion. Villages had been burnt but there were few or no dead. The villagers had fled into the mountains taking their livestock with them.

Another factor here was that the Egyptians were desert fighters and unused to fighting in the mountains. This made them vulnerable to ambush. The Greek shepherds were adepts of the sling and could knock a bird down at a hundred yards. A man presented a much larger target.

Antton held up a fist to stop the team and sank to a knee. The rest of them followed suit. He scanned the terrain around them watching for the slightest movement, but it was Garai who spotted it first.

"A local hiding behind a rock at ten o'clock."

Once they spotted one, they soon picked up the others. Antton stood, his arms held wide and faced one that was hidden above them.

"We come in peace," he said in Greek. A natural talent for language had helped him learn the basics of ancient Greek during the many hours of sailing.

A head appeared.

"Who are you?"

"Allies, we are here to find the Egyptian army and warn the fighters at Patras of their approach."

His Greek was slow and deliberate.

"Where are you from?" the head asked.

"We are with the British fleet that is stopping the Ottoman fleet from fighting. We are here to stop the war and give Greece independence."

The head dropped down and he could hear talking. It popped up again.

"Why should I believe you?"

"Because Bishop Germanos has blessed us and given us this."

Antton held up the silver and gold crucifix Marty had given them before they left.

**

They were taken to a camp in the hills where several villages had gathered. About a hundred men, women and children were there, mainly shepherds or farmers. Every man had a sling on his belt and so did more than a few women.

They sat around a fire with the leaders and ate a meal.

"The Egyptians are five miles away. They have stopped marching to try and find food. There are not so many towns they can loot up here in the mountains. and any near them have been evacuated and the food taken or destroyed."

Antton smiled at the way the Greeks were turning the Egyptians' own tactics against them.

"What about their supply trains?" he asked.

"Other groups ambush them. We use fire pots to set them on fire," a man called Lason told them, then rose and returned with a clay pot bound in a rope cradle. A rudimentary fuse stuck out the top. "We throw these at the carts. They are filled with oil, pitch and sulphur."

He demonstrated by lighting the fuse then whirling the pot around his head before launching it at a large rock some fifty yards away. The pot shattered and the rock was engulfed with fire.

"Effective," Antton said. "Can you show us where the Egyptians are?"

That evening they crossed the mountains to a valley where the Egyptian army was camped. It was full of campfires that lit the valley floor.

"How far are we from Patras?" Garai asked.

"Three days' march for us," Lason told them.

"And for them?"

"Five or six."

Antton looked at the camp thoughtfully.

"How far can you throw one of those fire pots?"

"About a hundred paces but with no accuracy."

Antton chuckled mirthlessly. "Accuracy won't be a problem."

**

A messenger was dispatched to the Greek army at Patras warning them of the Egyptian army's approach. Antton discussed tactics with the leaders.

"We can slow the enemy army down and weaken them without risking too many lives. What we need to do is…"

Before dawn twenty locals and the Shadows left the camp and made their way to the valley. When they got there, they could see the army preparing to march. Tents were broken down and the men were forming up in their units. Officers were mounting their horses and NCOs shouted orders. It looked disciplined.

They waited as the front ranks of the army started out. It took an hour for the rearmost echelon to start moving and they were followed by the baggage train. Antton smiled grimly, it was all working out as he expected. Their route would take them northeast through a pass.

Cavalry outriders flanked the army, patrolling as far out as they could before the slope got too steep. The Shadows moved to a point ahead of the column where the valley narrowed before emerging onto a plain. They set up on both sides and prepared their breech-loading rifles.

Behind the column the Greeks waited.

The first cavalry scouts passed through the pass, three minutes later the front rank of soldiers marched by. Antton waited until a column of what looked like heavy infantry armed with muskets appeared. He took aim at the officer leading them.

Bang! The officer fell and three more shots rang out as Matai, Chin and Garai fired. three more men fell, all officers and sergeants. Ten seconds later four more shots.

Antton moved, it didn't do for a sniper to stay in one place for more than a couple of shots. He settled and fired again into the ranks this time. His bullet took down two, passing through the neck of the first and side of the second. The others were firing at the same rate; six shots a minute, the conical bullets doing massive damage to whatever they hit.

The Egyptians thought they were under attack from a large group and dropped into a defensive formation returning fire with their muskets.

**

At the rear of the column, riders slid silently from their saddles felled by well-aimed sling stones. Men came out from behind rocks running forward to within a hundred yards of the baggage train. Pots whirled around their heads then arced through the air, trailing smoke.

The first pot smashed into the ground beside a cart and fire erupted in a wall, engulfing it. The carter screamed as he was set on fire and the horses bolted. More jars smashed, spreading fire through the baggage train. Horses and men screamed, and mayhem ensued.

**

Antton fired his tenth shot and grinned as he heard a rumbling explosion, his teeth white in his powder-stained face. He lifted his face to the sky and yelled, "Ayeee, Ayee, Ayee!" The Shadows slipped away leaving only the dead behind them.

They met up with the rest of the party in the hills well behind the Egyptian column. They could still see it and Antton passed around his telescope so all could get a look at their morning's work.

The column had made less than a mile's progress and was only now sorting itself out. The baggage train was very noticeably shorter and the cadre of cooks that were the last in line had been decimated.

"The powder wagon horses bolted into the middle of them before it blew up." Lason laughed.

The army moved out onto the plain and made camp. Guards surrounded it and the baggage train was moved right into the centre. Any brush or cover two hundred yards around the camp was cut down. Cavalry patrols in force were sent out and swept the area.

Antton thought it was all going swimmingly.

**

Men from the camp moved along the projected route of the army and warned every village that was five miles either side of it to take what they could and go up into the hills. Nothing was left that wasn't spoiled or poisoned. Silent villages greeted any Egyptian scavengers that found them. Fields were burnt and barns emptied. Not a goat, cow, chicken, donkey or sheep was to be found.

Scavengers were ambushed. A hail of deadly stones raining down on them launched by men and boys. Scavenging patrols got bigger and had to be escorted by cavalry. The Greeks hit and ran. The column slowed to less than five miles a day.

**

A messenger returned from Patras with an officer of the Greek army. They had resorted to blockading the main supply routes to Patras and there was no cogent target for the Egyptians to attack. The team could return to the fleet.

The Fleet Forms

The British Fleet had been patrolling the entrance to Navarino Bay in increasingly inclement weather for more than a week when one of the outlying frigates signalled the approach of a large formation of ships from the northwest. Marty knew that the only ships coming from that direction would be the Russians and/or French. Hopefully both.

He had to wait until his patrol identified that there were seven liners, six frigates and two schooners. It had to be both squadrons. This would lift his strength to twenty-six ships and a cutter.

He was surprised when he saw that Admiral Rigny's flag flew above the first-rank frigate the Sirèna, not the second-rate Breslaw. Admiral van Heiden's flag flew over the third-rate Azov as one would expect. The two admirals joined him on the Asia as soon as their squadrons fell into line.

"Gentlemen, welcome," Marty greeted them after they were piped aboard with all due ceremony. Both spoke excellent English which was good as while Marty spoke fluent French, he hardly knew a word of Russian and only a little Dutch. He was also gratified to see that the two men actually seemed to get on, contrary to the rumours he had been spreading.

Rigney was particularly interested in the ship as she was relatively new and built in India.

"She is a fine ship, is she made of oak?"

"Teak, eighty-four guns. She is just three years old. I see your flag on the Sirèna."

Rigney looked a little chagrined. "She was my flagship prior to this mission, and I thought about moving it to the Breslaw. However, I must be candid and say that I have seen ships in better condition than the three that were sent to me."

"They can fight if needed?"

"Yes, they can do that much."

The Russians had sent the three-year-old Gangut, an eighty-four-gun third rate and three relatively new eighty-gun second rates, the Azov, Lezekill and Aleksandr Nevsjii along with four frigates.

They sat together in Marty's day room.

"We are facing an Ottoman fleet of three third rates, nine double-decked frigates, eight single-decked frigates, thirty corvettes, five schooners, twenty-eight brigs and half a dozen fireships."

Rigney looked at his fellow admirals wryly,

"All trained by my colleagues no doubt."

Marty nodded.

"Yes, last time I was aboard the Fahti Bahri there were still a lot of French advisors aboard."

"I will talk to them. They will not want to fight their own."

Van Heiden looked slightly bemused, so Rigney clarified for him.

"My government and the king are very much for the Ottomans and Egypt. However, the French people are very much inspired by the Greek's struggle for independence. We French enjoy a good rebellion."

The others laughed at his wit, and he continued.

"So, my reluctant government complied with the Letter of the Treaty by sending their oldest ships to join my squadron of frigates and schooners while trumpeting their support to the masses. Thereby staving off another revolution at home."

"You think there will be one?" Marty asked.

"Probably, hardly anyone likes the Bourbons and Napoleon set the idea of a republic in people's minds."

Marty made a mental note to keep a close eye on France in the future but for now they were allies.

**

The weather worsened making it harder to blockade the bay. Marty made repeated attempts to contact Ibrahim and even sent James in as his envoy.

James sailed the Talbot into the bay under a white flag noting the close attention the battery on Sphacelaria Island paid to him. He dipped his flag in salute to the fortress on the mainland and again to the flagship. He took a boat across to it and was greeted at the entry port by a lieutenant.

"What do you want?" the man said in French, a line of soldiers behind him that were not there for ceremonial purposes.

"I wish to speak to Ibrahim Pasha. I have a message from my admiral," James replied in kind.

"Give it to me, I will pass it to him."

"I cannot. My orders are quite explicit; I must give it to him personally."

"He is not here."

"His flag is flying," James pointed out.

"The admiral is not here." The lieutenant signalled the soldiers who advanced their bayoneted muskets.

"Very well, pass him this message. My Lord Admiral Stockley wishes to hold urgent talks to avoid further conflict."

"I will tell him when I see him," the lieutenant sneered.

**

James reported back to Marty who was in conference with the other admirals.

"They wouldn't let me see him. I was told he was not there."

"Our adversary is conspicuous by his absence," Rigny quipped. "May I try and send my flag lieutenant over?"

"We should try all measures," van Heiden agreed.

"Certainly, give it a shot," Marty agreed.

Two hours later the lieutenant returned disappointed.

**

By the seventeenth of October the weather had degraded to the point that blockade was impossible, and Marty called the allied commanders together again.

"Gentlemen, we have to decide what to do next. The Ottomans and their allies are still burning Greek villages and Ibrahim is refusing to talk to us."

"Whatever we do we should all agree on," van Heiden said.

"I have an idea, may I put it to you?" Marty said and walked to a large-scale map of the bay pinned on a board. He had marked the disposition of the Imperial Squadron on it.

"Ibrahim has deployed his liners and large frigates in a line here along the coast from the fortress down to the road to Messena. They are backed by a second row of his next most powerful ships and a third of his smallest. He has positioned his fire ships at either end of his line." He looked at them to see if they had understood.

"That looks like the work of my countrymen," Rigny observed.

"We have two options. One is to abandon the blockade leaving only a couple of frigates and retire to Zantos. The other, and my preferred option, is to sail into the bay and set up in a peaceful line. That will send the message that we are not to put off."

"A very strong message," Rigny agreed, ever the diplomat. "What if they interpret it as a threat?"

"Then they start a fight they will not win," van Heiden stated firmly.

"We could be accused of being provocative," Marty said, playing devil's advocate.

"And Ibrahim is not? He is burning the Greeks out of house and home!" van Heiden snapped.

"Gentlemen, we must approach this without passion," Rigny chided.

Marty looked from one to the other.

"I agree, but if we sail away Ibrahim will have won this round. Can we in all conscience do that?"

The two men looked thoughtful then shook their heads.

"Then we must decide how to enter the bay and our disposition."

They discussed it and finally agreed.

"I will enter first and anchor in line with this small island. The French ships will drop in, in line behind us and finally the Russian squadron opposite the castle. "

"If it comes to a fight, I will be caught between the battery on Sphaeleria and the castle," van Heiden observed.

Marty smiled. "Do not worry, the battery will not present a threat if it comes to a battle. My men will neutralise it."

**

On the twentieth, at one thirty in the afternoon the combined fleet entered the bay with the ships at quarters just in case. Quietly and without ceremony they advanced to their positions and anchored. Marty finally received a message from Ibrahim telling him that he had not given permission for the allies to enter the bay. Marty replied that it was not his bay but the Greeks and he had come to enforce the Treaty of London. He also warned that he would destroy the Ottoman fleet if they opened fire.

Marty evaluated his position and the relative strengths of the two fleets. On paper he looked to be outnumbered two to one in guns. He had one thousand, two hundred and fifty-eight guns against their two thousand, one hundred and eighty. However, that ignored several key points. He had more front-line vessels with ten ships of the line against Ibrahim's three. That was offset by the seven double-decked frigates on the Ottoman side. His guns were newer and bigger than the opposition, His gunners better trained and he could count on delivering two broadsides for every one of theirs.

Ibrahim had a lot of smaller ships but against the liners they were pretty much useless. They could give his frigates a hard time if they mobbed them but manoeuvring in the bay would be near impossible.

His biggest fear was the fire ships. If they could be brought into operation, they could endanger his liners. He ordered the Dartmouth, along with two brigs and four schooners, to keep watch on the corvettes and fire ships on the Ottoman left. Then he remembered the French officers acting as shadow captains to the Egyptians. They needed to be removed from the equation.

**

Henri de Rigy read the note Marty had sent across to his ship. The English admiral was right to point out that there were still French officers aboard the Egyptian ships. He decided to go and talk to their senior officer personally.

Captain Jean-Mark Letellier was based on the Egyptian flagship and had been largely responsible for devising the defensive formation that they had adopted. When Rigny found him, he was in bed sick with a fever.

"How ill are you?" Rigny asked, covering his nose and mouth with a handkerchief.

"I feel like I am dying." Letellier was grey and shivering.

"You need to order your men off the Egyptian ships. There is every likelihood that there will be a battle and I do not want to fight my countrymen."

"We can move to the Austrian Brig; it is a neutral."

"Ha! In name only," Rigny scoffed.

Letellier asked for paper and a pen and wrote an order.

"Give this to my lieutenant and he will take care of the rest." He was wracked by coughing and Rigny beat a hasty retreat.

**

Marty saw the boats ferry the French from the Egyptian ships to the Austrian Brig which purposely moved away from the Ottoman fleet to a spot some way down the bay. Now he considered what to do about those fire ships.

The Battle of Navarino Bay

As the fleet anchored, Marty ordered the ship's band to begin playing as a sign that their intentions were peaceful. By a quarter after two the liners were in place. In a pause in the music, he heard the trumpeters aboard the Ottoman's vessels calling their ships to action stations.

Disappointed, Marty sent the Shadows to neutralise the battery on the island.

"If possible do not kill anyone unless a general engagement starts at which time you can take the gloves off and just do what you have to."
**

At the entrance to the bay, Captain Fellows of the Dartmouth, noticed that one of the fire ships was being prepared. Ships were still moving into the bay so he said, "Mr Fitzroy, would you be so kind as to take a boat and ask those fellows to desist in getting that fire ship ready for sea."

Fitzroy, the fifth lieutenant and most junior ran to do as he was bid. The boat was rowed across. He stood in the bow with a white flag.

"I say, you fellows," he called.

The Ottomans immediately and without warning opened fire with muskets mortally wounding the young lieutenant and several of the crew who beat a hasty retreat. Fellows saw this and instructed his musketeers to fire back to give covering fire. The Ottomans set fire to the fire ship.

"Dammit, are they mad? Get the cutter over there and tow the damn thing away," Fellows cried.

The cutter was fired on as soon as it closed, and more casualties were inflicted. The Dartmouth's marines opened fire again to give cover. At the same time the French flagship the Sirène, which was passing behind the Dartmouth, opened fire with muskets in support.

From such minor instances wars are begun. One of the Ottoman corvettes that supported the fire ships opened fire with her main guns on the Sirène. This caused a chain reaction along the Ottoman line which in a massive ripple opened fire on the allies.

The ship behind the Sirène, the Scipion, third rate of eighty guns, immediately came under attack from Egyptian frigates from all sides along with the shore batteries. An Ottoman fire ship was deployed and got jammed under her bowsprit. The crew of the Scipion threw themselves on the flames to stop them spreading to the forward powder magazine. Their gallant action saved the ship and bought time for the Trident to get a line onto the fire ship and tow her away with the assistance of the Dartmouth's boats. The cost was great; many gallant men suffered horrendous burns and would take no more part in the fighting that day.

**

On shore the Shadows had just landed and hearing the musket fire broke into a run to get to the shore battery. Before they got there the battery was already engaging the Scipion. The noise of the guns effectively covered their approach.

Antton signalled Garai, Sam and Chin to circle around to the four-gun battery's right flank, while he, Adam and Matai would attack from the right. At one hundred yards Adam dropped to the ground and took up his rifle to snipe the gunners. Chin did the same on the other flank. The other Shadows would advance under cover of that fire taking shots as targets presented themselves.

Adam chose his first target. An officer that was directing fire. He waited until the guns fired and shot him through the turban. Chin took out a gunner bringing a fresh cartridge to the gun. As they reloaded, the others fired and advanced as skirmishers.

The gunners took a long moment to discover they were under fire as the Shadows chose targets at the back like a hunter would shoot a skein of geese. By the time they realised what was going on the Shadows were amongst them and dealing out death indiscriminately. As soon as the boys were engaged Chin rushed in to join them, butterfly swords flashing in the weak afternoon sunshine. Adam kept up a regular fire, picking off men who tried to attack his comrades from behind.

It was over in minutes; the dead lying around their guns. Antton found a hammer amongst the tools lying around the battery and took four steel pins from his pouch and hammered one in each of the gun's touchholes – effectively disabling them.

**

Marty saw the ripple approach and ordered, "Raise the engage, run out and return fire." He knew that not all his ships were in position. The Asia was anchored between the Ottoman, Admiral Capitan Bey's flagship, Fahti Bahri, and the Guerrière, a sixty-gun frigate captained by Moharram Bey.

The Fahti Bahri opened fire but a boat approached from the other ship and shouted up that the Guerrière would not fight.

"Concentrate your fire on the Fahti Bahri!" Marty ordered.

His gunners went to work with a will; the broadside rippling along her side. Curzon and Baynes urged the men on and managed a broadside every minute or so. Soon smoke obscured the target and only her gun flashes were visible faintly through the smoke. They judged their progress by the number and rate of fire.

On her own, the Ottoman was seriously outgunned, but all the smaller ships anchored behind the two lines of battleships opened fire through the gap between the two vessels. The Asia was taking damage and casualties. Marty saw the damage and heard the screams of the wounded, but he had to keep his resolve and finish this. Eventually there were no flashes from the direction of the flagship and Marty asked Curzon to have his men raise their aim to send shot into the second and third rows of smaller ships.

With the flagship destroyed, the corvettes decided that discretion was the better part of valour and stopped their bombardment.

Marty called for the Greek interpreter he had onboard.

"Mr Mikelis, would you be so kind as to take a boat over to the Guerrière and parlay a peaceful settlement with Capitan Bey."

"Certainly, Admiral," the scholarly man said, keen to do his bit.

The boat rowed across and hooked on. Mikelis climbed the side as Marty watched through a telescope. As he reached the deck he suddenly arched backwards and fell into the boat. He had barely landed when the Guerrière opened fire.

"You cowardly bastard," Marty snarled as the boat was being rowed frantically clear of the ship.

"Blow her out of the water!" he cried and the guns spoke.

The Russian flagship, Azov, had sailed up to provide support to the Asia and lent her guns to the battle. The two reduced the Guerrière to a burning wreck in twenty minutes.

**

In the centre the Albion dropped her anchor and opened fire on an Ottoman frigate. She was joined by the Azov who had left the Asia to her repairs. The large frigate soon became another hulk, smashed to pieces by the overwhelming firepower of two ships of the line. Albion now became the focus of the other Ottoman ships of the line and heavy frigates.

My God, they couldn't hit a cow's arse with a paddle," captain John Acworth Ommanney laughed at the inept performance of the Ottoman gunners. He and the Azov were joined by the Breslaw, the French eighty-four, captained by Captain Botherel de la Bretonnière, as both ships were hard pressed despite the lack of the Ottoman gunner's skill. The fight was hot, and the Asia joined in, swinging around on her springs to bring her main battery to bear, Ottoman corvettes fired between their liners in support as the big ship's broadsides flew back and forth. Men died on both sides but, importantly, more on the Ottoman ships.

After two hours with all the allied line of battleships engaged the three Ottoman ships of the line were destroyed. This left the smaller ships at their mercy. The fire of battle coursed through the captain's veins, and they fired on them without mercy.

**

The Sirène, in the meantime, was attacked by the Ishania, a sixty-four-gun frigate. The ships exchanged broadsides at close range inflicting severe damage to each other.

Rigny urged his gunners on to fire as fast as they could from their long twenty-fours. However, it was the twenty-two, twenty-four-pound carronades they carried that won the duel. A smasher entered the Ishania's magazine which exploded destroying the ship. Though severely damaged Rigny ordered that they bombard Navarino Castle which was lying down a steady fire of heated shot. The Trident joined them, and they set about silencing the shore guns. Her thirty-two-pound lower deck guns tore the battlements apart as they systematically blasted the castle to pieces.

**

Out on the Ottoman left flank the Russians were the last to take up station because the Azov had been supporting the British ships in the centre. This was a most intense area of fighting where most of the big Ottoman frigates supported by corvettes, briggs and schooners were stationed.

Van Heiden was in for the fight of his life. He took on the flagship of Hassen Bey of the Tunis Squadron which was joined by elements of the Alexandria Squadron. He found himself facing three large frigates simultaneously and having to fight both sides of his ship as they tried to surround him.

The Russian gunners were good and the Asov's hull strong. She sank or disabled them all and a corvette but took one hundred and fifty-three hits in return. Incredibly the casualties on the Russian side were not as high as van Heiden first feared. However, the casualties and deaths on the Ottoman side were horrific.

**

James in the Talbot and the French frigate Armide commanded by Captain Hugon were positioned on the Ottoman right wing, facing not only ships but a shore battery as well.

"Let them have it, boys," he cried and steered the Talbot close where his carronades could do their worst.

His gunners responded, ignoring the hail of shot that was incoming. If a man went down, he was dragged away and replaced by another. Smoke obscured everything and they fired at the flashes of guns rather than at ships they could not see. Screams could be heard all around them as they pounded away. A gust of wind parted the smoke in time for James to spot an Ottoman corvette trying to get across his bow.

"Fore chasers, fire!"

As soon as the guns fired, he spun the wheel to bring his starboard battery to bear, his helmsman having been taken below with a musket ball in his shoulder. The gunners needed no telling, firing as they bore, ripping the smaller ship to matchwood.

They were being overwhelmed, casualties mounting, rigging shot to hell when two Russian frigates arrived. The ninety-two extra guns the

Provornyl and Konstantine brought to the fight made all the difference. The Talbot, all but disabled as her masts and rigging were shot to pieces and half her guns disabled, anchored and targeted the shore battery with the remaining guns.

James was hit by a piece of shrapnel in the thigh and had to use a rammer as a crutch to remain standing. He refused to leave his post until the shore battery had been silenced. The two-inch piece of iron was removed by the surgeon who operated in James's cabin while he was still conscious. A leather strap between his teeth, his only succour. Once it was removed and he was stitched up he took a large glass of brandy up to the quarterdeck and sat in a canvas chair to oversee the repairs as his first had also been wounded.

**

It was not all about the line of battleships and big frigates. The fleet's smaller ships played a crucial role as well. The brigs and schooners under the direction of the Dartmouth were responsible for countering the fire ship threat. The four nimble ten gunners bravely intercepted and towed away any that were moving against the line, sinking them out of harm's way. Not one got through, much to their credit.

Marty noted after the battle that, "The smallest of our ships distinguished themselves today and suffered casualties in proportion as great as the larger ships."

**

By four o'clock Marty decided that they had done enough and signalled the cease fire. However, there was so much smoke that no one could see it, or they ignored it as their blood was up. Consequently, the fighting continued and turned into a massacre as the second and third lines of Ottoman ships came under the guns of the liners and big frigates.

By dusk, two hours later, almost all the Ottoman fleet had been destroyed or disabled despite the singular bravery of the Ottoman crews, who, rather than let them be captured, either burnt or scuttled their disabled ships. In reality three quarters were sunk, the rest destroyed by their crews.

Silence fell as the sun dipped to the horizon, only the groans of the wounded disturbed the silence. Marty walked the deck of the Asia stepping over pieces of rigging and broken deck planking. The smoke blew away and the full measure of their afternoon's work could be seen. Marty shook his head, what a waste. He comforted a wounded man then climbed up an undamaged rat line to view his fleet. His eye settled on the Talbot. She was a mess but her men were swarming over the rigging making repairs. He looked for James and found him on the quarterdeck. Relief flowed through him and he sucked in a huge breath as he was almost overcome. He climbed down and returned to the quarterdeck.

"What is that?" Curzon said.

Marty cocked his head to one side, trying to hear above the ringing in his ears from the constant roar of the guns.

"It's bells, church bells. They are ringing the victory," Marty said.

He was right. The news was spreading across the Peloponnese and to the rest of Greece like wildfire. People came out of their houses to the sound of the church bells ringing, hearing that the mighty Ottoman fleet had been annihilated, and the Greek nation had been saved. The rejoicing was wild and unbridled, continuing throughout the night.

Large bonfires were built on the peaks of the mountains in the Peloponnese and Mount Pamassos in central Greece sending the message to all who could see them. Even the occupied regions celebrated with the now demoralised invaders sulking in their fortresses.

**

Marty slept little that night. Reports came in from the ships of the fleet and had to be digested and acted upon. The butcher's bill when he had added it up came to one hundred and eighty-one dead, four hundred and eighty wounded. That was an enormous cost and it sat heavily on his conscience. Not only that, but all of his liners needed extensive repairs with the Russian ships Azov, Gangut and Lezekill disabled, but not a single allied ship had been sunk.

All of his fleet needed repairs before they could sail again and his men needed rest. He wrote his report, praising the men and naming individuals who had distinguished themselves. He did this on the quarterdeck as the transom windows of his cabin had been shot out and the head had acquired a new porthole. He had no ship's boats either, they had all been destroyed in the fight.

"Admiral, may I interrupt?" a lieutenant who he did not recognise said.

"What is it Mr?"

"Acting Sixth Lieutenant Wade, Sir. Captain Curzon's compliments, Sir. He requests permission to use some of the enemy ships for spares."

"Granted. How is he going to retrieve them? I thought all the boats were gone."

"A hatch cover and empty water casks, Sir."

"A raft, good idea." Marty went back to writing his report.

**

The resulting report was a massive tome incorporating all the reports from his captains. It took his clerk a day and a half to make the required copies.

Someone had found a fishing boat that was requisitioned until his crew had time to construct a new barge. He went around the fleet starting with the Russians. He climbed aboard the Azov which was a patchwork of plugs and new timbers. The sound of saws, adzes and hammers echoed around the deck.

"Good morning, Lodewijk," Marty said in Dutch.

"Good morning, Martin," Lodewijk replied and shook the proffered hand.

Marty switched to English.

"My God you took a battering."

"She is no longer a new ship and a virgin." Lodewijk laughed.

"You have buried your dead?"

"The men wish to be buried at home so the officers are preserved in brandy casks and the men buried temporarily in the ballast."

Marty nodded, that had been common practice in the British fleet in the previous century. There was a Russian Orthodox priest prowling the deck like a black bat.

"We will bury ours at sea, luckily it's autumn so not so hot."

Marty looked at the priest and Lodewijk commented conspiratorially.

"He looks like the angel of death but the men like having him aboard. Personally, I could do without any priests on my ships."

The two stood in companionable silence for a while.

"How is your son? I heard he was wounded," Lodewijk said.

"He is recovering well. He got a two-inch lump of iron in his thigh. It came out no trouble and the surgeon stitched him up."

Lodewijk nodded. He did not have to mention the danger of rot. Marty knew of it well enough.

**

The Sirène was his next stop where he found Henri de Rigny with his arm in a sling.

"Bonjour, Henri, how is your wing?"

"It is good, no corruption and the skin is pink and healthy."

Marty looked around the ship. The crew had repaired about half of the damage.

"Will you be able to sail to Toulon?" Marty asked, knowing it was their home base.

"We should be fine. What about your ships?"

"The liners will manage to limp to Portsmouth for repairs. The smaller ships will go to Malta then resume patrolling the Ionian Sea."

"And you my friend?"

"I will stay within the Mediterranean as is my duty unless I am recalled." As Marty said it, he remembered James Turner and knew he wouldn't be there for long.

Aftermath

The British fleet returned to Malta, the Russian to Kaliningrad as the Ottomans would not allow them through the Bosphorus into the Black Sea, the French to Toulon.

The British dead were buried in the Ionian Sea with great ceremony. Marty switched his flag to the Glasgow and the liners made their way home. His report and the fleet's letters went by fast packet and would get to England well ahead of the lumbering liners.

James visited and they met in his cabin.

"Let me see your wound," Marty said as James was still using a cane to get around.

James knew there was no point in arguing and dropped his trousers.

Marty examined it, the surgeon had done a decent job. Closing it with a row of twelve fine stitches. The drain was still in place.

"Is it still draining?"

"It stopped yesterday."

The flesh was pink and healthy with no sign of corruption. Satisfied Marty had him replace his trousers.

"Have you heard from Mother?" James asked.

"Only letters that are two weeks old. They will not have heard about the battle yet. I wrote to her, Beth and the twins."

"Yes, I wrote to them and Melissa. I don't want them worrying."

Marty barked a laugh.

"The twins are too wrapped up in their careers to notice something going on in this part of the world. Beth is in South America again and it will be months before the letters get there."

"True but Mother and Melissa will care. So, you don't have new orders yet?"

"No, there was nothing waiting for me here."

**

There were three drydocks in Valletta and they were all in use as first the large frigates and then the smaller ships could be repaired and refitted. Marty planned to take the first three frigates out on patrol once they were swimming again but that wouldn't be for several weeks.

The governor invited him to dinner and he had time to spend with Veronica and Billy to catch up on the latest intelligence from inside Greece and from new agents they had recruited in Egypt and Constantinople.

"The Ottomans still have some forty thousand men in Greece and Mahmud II is still determined to subdue it," Veronica reported. "Frances says that the Greeks are going to go for full independence and not what it says in the Treaty."

"That's to be expected now the Ottomans are without a fleet." Marty looked at the big map of the eastern Mediterranean on the wall. "I wonder how long it will be before the Russians declare war on them."

"Not long, you have severely weakened them."

"It wasn't my intention but as these things do, it escalated very quickly. Ibrahim made a bad misjudgement thinking they could beat us."

The fast packet arrived with the mail. It was six weeks since the battle. Marty had the usual admiralty communiques and a sealed packet. He read it and called his officers together.

"Gentlemen, I have been recalled to London and will leave as soon as my replacement arrives. Admiral Codrington is an experienced man with a fine record."

There was a flurry of questions. Marty held up his hands.

"I am being given a role in government." He did not say that it was the role vacated by James Turner's death as the head of the Foreign and Overseas desk of British Intelligence. "And I am to report to parliament on the action as there seems to be a faction that think what we have done was unnecessary and reckless. Luckily they are vocal but a minority."

The captains to a man, vowed to support him. One or two who knew about his involvement with the Intelligence Service had an inkling what the government position would be. They ate dinner with him and toasted his health. James was quiet.

After the meal Marty asked him to stay for a moment.

"What is wrong?"

"Melissa is on her way here."

"And that is a problem?"

"I am concerned about what the other officers will think."

"They will be jealous for sure but they will not blame you. This is your home port for now and having one's wife nearby is only natural.

Your mother would take any opportunity to be nearby. Has she loaned Melissa the Pride?"

**

Codrington arrived in a new eighty-four a week later around the same time as Melissa in the Pride. Marty took advantage of that and as soon as he could took the Pride back to England. James and Melissa would have all the time they needed to catch up as the Talbot would not be refitted until after her big sisters had been completed.

The Pride moored at the Stockley family wharf in India Dock and Marty went ashore. A carriage was waiting, and Caroline threw herself into his arms from the top step. The kiss was long and full of promise. His sea bags loaded and the Shadows were either on top or astride the horses as they set off for home.

"What has been the reaction to the battle here?" Marty asked.

"The majority of the people rejoiced. There is something romantic about Greece being freed from the shackles of the Ottoman Empire. The newspapers have been trumpeting about the atrocities the Ottomans and Egyptians have committed and how the fleet has aided them. Somehow they found out that the Ottomans fired the first shot."

Marty smiled sardonically.

"That would be Arthur's doing, there is significant opposition to any intervention on our part. Not enough to cause long standing issues but able to make life difficult for the government."

Caroline snorted in contempt.

"Robinson is weak. Arthur should take over."

Marty smiled, "He will in good time."

**

Waiting for him at home was his appointment as Head of the Foreign and Overseas Branch of British Intelligence reporting to Arthur Wellesley. There was also a summons to appear before a house committee looking into the conduct of the battle.

"That didn't take long," Caroline said.

"Probably want to get it out of the way."

Marty had a week to settle back in and the first thing he did was to go to Greenwich and visit the grave of his friend. A handsome tombstone marked the grave which had his honours engraved on a cartouche at the top.

"Old friend, I will miss you and your wisdom. I never really thanked you for all you did for me because without you I would probably be pushing up daisies in a pauper's grave down in Purbeck. You took a raw boy and made him into something quite different. You should have had the knighthood, not me."

Marty knelt and took a badge of the Order of the Bath and placed it on the grave where James's chest should lie. He covered it with a stone.

**

He visited his office. It was strange not having to be given permission by the clerk in the foyer to enter the building and to get a touch of the forelock from him as he passed. The office was pretty much as James would have left it, except his personal belongings were gone. Marty sat at the desk and looked around the room. It felt empty.

The door to the secretary's office opened and Ezra Browning stuck his head through the door.

"I thought I heard you enter, Sir. Can I get you coffee?"

"Yes please, Ezra. Is there anything urgent that needs looking at?"

"Well, Sir, Admiral Turner left instructions for me for when he passed the job onto you. If you look in the top right-hand drawer there is a letter from him which he asked that you read first."

Marty opened the drawer and saw a bunch of keys sitting on top of an envelope. He removed both and used a switchblade from his pocket to slit the envelope open.

My dear friend and colleague

You are sitting in my chair now and I must say you are the only person I would trust with it. The first thing I would say is that this does not mean you will have to sail a desk for the rest of your life. How you run the department is up to you.

Do not let the bureaucrats and politicians dictate what you do. Your task is to be independent of them all and do what is for the good of the country. That might mean you have to go against government policy and investigate a friendly power or eliminate a threat within that power.

I have bequeathed you a network of formidable agents and operatives. Get to know them. Ezra has their files prepared. Talking of Ezra, he is not getting any younger and deserves a period of retirement. He is an avid gardener and should be given a small plot to supplement his garden. Get a younger man in as his assistant so he can train him.

Ezra came in with the coffee and poured Marty a cup. Marty took notice of him for probably the first time and saw an old man.

"Anything else, Sir?"

"No, that will be all for now, thank you."

Wellington is likely to become Prime Minister in the new year. If he does then George Hamilton will be Foreign Secretary and your superior. Hamilton is not a pacifist, though many think he is, he has an aversion to war but is quite capable of supporting one if he thinks it is needed. What he does do well is get close to the ambassadors of other countries but that has its own dangers and you must protect him from himself in these cases.

His main problems will be Greece, French and American relations, and the slave trade. I warn you not to take your eye off the other main players either. Russia, the Ottomans, Egypt, the Spanish, Portuguese, Netherlands and Belgium all want a piece of our trade. Then there is the ongoing strife in South America. In short, the world is your oyster.

I send my love to Caroline and your children. Your faithful friend.

Marty sat back and picked up his coffee. Adam would make an excellent clerk. He had a fine writing hand but would hate copying out orders so would need a copyist. His organisational skills were exceptional, and he had a keen mind. That decided he turned his mind to the rest of the Shadows. They would all make excellent instructors at the academy, except Roland who Caroline would want to keep on as their chef. However, Matai and Sam were both married to members of the household. He decided they should stay as his security detail. He would ask Garai, Chin and Antton to instruct at the academy.

There was a knock in the door and Arthur Wellesley stuck his head around. "I heard you were in the building."

"Come in, I was just having a look around."

The tall stately figure of the Duke of Wellington was imposing, and he had a naturally superior look, partly due to his eagle's beak of a nose. Marty, however, knew him better.

"How are the boys?" Marty asked and called for another cup.

"Splendid," Arthur smiled.

The boys were Arthur's pride and joy. He and his wife Kitty had mostly lived apart since the second was born in 1808 with Kitty living in their Stratford Saye house while Arthur lived in their London home, Apsley House in Piccadilly. Marty knew Arthur had a string of extramarital relationships and that his current interest was an actress.

"I will want to bring in Adam and a copyist to eventually replace Ezra who is due for retirement," Marty said.

"Have you told Ezra yet?" Arthur said with a snort of mirth.

Marty smiled. "No, not yet but I will gift him a patch of land, he is a keen gardener."

"James's idea, no doubt."

Arthur sobered and changed the subject to more important matters.

"You have been summoned before the committee?"

"I have, next week on Wednesday."

"Gambier is the chair."

Marty's eyebrows went up. "Is he, bedamned."

Marty and Admiral Gambier had history. They did not like each other at all and had largely kept out of each other's way since the Battle of the Basque Roads in '08.

"Yes, and half of the committee are his supporters," Arthur added sipping his coffee. "He will try to needle you into losing your temper. Here is your protection."

Arthur passed a folded sheet of paper to Marty who opened it. His eyebrows rose in surprise before tucking it into his coat pocket.

**

The committee was held in a room of the Palace of Westminster and Marty sat in an anteroom waiting to be called. He wore his uniform and all his honours. He read the latest copy of *The Times* which he had purchased on his way in.

"Admiral Stockley? The committee will see you now," a steward said.

Marty folded his paper, left it on the table and got sedately to his feet. He followed the steward into the committee room to a chair that had been set in front of a line of men behind a committee table.

He sat without being told to and crossed his legs, brushing an imaginary speck of lint from his trouser leg.

"Good morning, mister chairman, good morning gentlemen. How may I help you?"

Gambier flushed at the lack of formal greeting. Marty outranked him socially even if the admiral outranked him in the navy.

"Vice Admiral Stockley," Gambier opened emphasising the word, Vice. "Your manners seem to need sharpening."

"I am sorry, Admiral; I was under the understanding this is a political committee not a naval one." Marty smiled.

Someone at the end snickered which made Gambier flush even more.

"Please explain your unnecessary provocation of the Ottoman fleet at Navarino!" Gambier snapped.

"That would indicate that you have already made your mind up, Admiral. Can I have your assurance that you will be impartial in this matter?"

Gambier opened his mouth to snap back an answer when a hand came to rest on his arm and Lord Fellows, who sat next to him and was a long-term supporter of Gambier, said, "We can assure you that this committee is only seeking the facts and is not prejudging anything."

Marty nodded in acknowledgement. "Would the chairman like to restate his question?"

Gambier physically pulled himself together and asked, "Admiral, would you kindly tell us the circumstances and thoughts that led you to take the combined fleet into Navarino Bay."

Marty calmly told of the storm, his discussions with the Russian and French admirals and how they came to the decision.

"Admiral," Thomas James, a Tory member said, "so, the decision was made in consultation with the other admirals."

"Yes, but ultimately as Commander in Chief it was my responsibility to make the final decision."

Gambier gloated.

"So, you admit to being responsible for what can only be perceived as a provocative and foolhardy gesture."

Marty looked at him long and hard.

"Sir, if making a move intended to confine the Ottoman combined fleet in accordance with my orders, when the alternative was to set them loose to continue their depravations of the Greek people, is considered by you as foolhardy, I admit to making the decision. I do not have the gift of foresight so could not possibly anticipate the turn of events that unfolded nor was I prepared to sit on my arse and do nothing."

That was the second point scored by Marty in the eyes of the non-partisan members.

Lord Fellows asked the next question.

"Can you tell us in your own words what happened next?"

"I sent several messages to Ibrahim Bey requesting a meeting, none of which he replied to. I then sent a note informing him that I would enter the bay and that we would not fire unless fired upon."

"Those were the orders to your captains?" Gambier asked.

"They were and in writing."

"Please continue," Fellows said.

Marty told of how Lieutenant Fitzroy went to ask the Ottomans to stop preparing their fire ships as that was seen as endangering the fleet and how he was shot and killed. He spoke with passion about the brave young man who was unarmed and died doing his duty. He told how he had gazetted him for his actions.

"The whole thing escalated in seconds after that. The Ottomans fired on the boat, wounding several of the crew. The Dartmouth's marines provided covering fire for their retreat with the French flagship, the Sirène, also providing support with muskets."

"That is when the first cannon shot was fired?" Fellows asked.

"Yes, one of the corvettes that was in support of the fire ships fired her broadside at the Sirène which triggered the whole Ottoman fleet to open fire."

"By God, Sir! This could all have been avoided!" Gambier barked.

Marty decided he needed to stop him in his tracks.

"You know? I had the same thought and have struggled with my conscience ever since. I even talked to a man of God. One who you know quite well, the vicar of St Peter's. Nice man, strange he is still single." He looked directly into Gambier's eyes as he said it, his expression one that said, do not mess with me.

Gambier's face turned from white to pink and back to white.

After a few more questions, Marty was thanked and allowed to go. He stood and bowed to the committee and treated Gambier to a smile and a wink.

The Ionian Patrol

The Talbot was brought into the drydock along with the Rose, the dock being big enough to take them both at the same time. All her damaged timbers were removed and replaced along with any damaged knees. Her ribs were in good shape, miraculously none had been hit. Her patched and temporary rigging had been removed before she had been towed into the drydock by a small steam tugboat.

James was fascinated by the powerful little sidewheeler and took time to visit it and look around the engines and mechanisms. *What a wonderful age we live in,* he marvelled at the hissing steaming engine. It was quieter than he had imagined; the only noise coming from the escaping steam and the roar of the fire when the doors were opened.

He imagined sailing against the wind towards an enemy who was constrained by the elements and wondered why the powers were not investing in steam-powered battleships. He had to admit that coal dust and smoke made everything dirty, which was anathema to any navy officer, but that was an inconvenience he would be prepared to live with.

The Talbot's hull was repaired and re-coppered, her broken guns replaced, and she was floated out of the drydock. New masts were stepped and rigging installed.

"She's as good as new!" Ed Pascoe grinned as he came onto the quarterdeck.

James agreed with him but kept his thoughts to himself, he would see how she sailed first. New canvas was being brought aboard on the starboard side and shot on the port. The last stores would be food, fuel and water.

His biggest problem was he was short of men. He had started out with one hundred and eighty-nine men, most of which were rated able with only twenty or so landsmen. Eighteen men had been killed and another twenty-seven were languishing in the hospital on shore. The accepted minimum for a ship of the Talbot's size was one hundred and fifty the maximum two hundred and forty including the marines.

"We need more able hands."

Ed shrugged. "The fifth rates have taken up all the available men on the island and we cannot press men anymore."

James could see no way out. His orders were to re-join the squadron as soon as he was replenished. Gibraltar was too far away and Minorca, though only two days hard sailing away and a port that the British used, was in part of Spain.

"Send out handbills that we are recruiting and have Mr Harris and the mids scour the bars for anyone willing to pull on a rope."
**

They were about to sail, having only filled a half dozen places, when the Pride of Purbeck sailed into harbour. James was surprised to see her and even more surprised when she pulled up alongside. Captain Dunbar stepped aboard and gestured to a large group of men gathered on the Pride's main deck.

"Compliments of your father," he said and beckoned the men to come aboard. "Every one of them able."

James did a headcount – twenty men! That would help enormously.

"He asked for volunteers from the holding ships and got these. Some are only just made but they all have some sea time. He suggests that if you need more to ask Captain Ackermann for a few men. The SOF is being recalled but I can delay the delivery of the orders until you have talked to him."

James shook his head, there was not a bad man aboard the SOF's ships. He thanked Dunbar for his help and suggested they should sail to Zante together with the Rose as they were ready to sail.

The trip was pleasant enough. The weather, unseasonably calm, with a fresh breeze from the south. The ships made good progress and pulled into Zante to find the flagship and fifth rates there, anchored beside the SOF ships.

James reported directly to Admiral Codrington while Ed Pascoe took a letter over to Wolfgang Ackermann on the Unicorn. James was taken directly to the admiral's cabin on arrival.

"Captain Stockley, you made good time. Is your ship fit for action?"

James glanced out of the stern window and saw a pair of boats pulling away from the Unicorn.

"It is, Sir."

"You have enough men?"

"Yes, Sir," he replied absolutely straight faced, "we recruited some in Malta."

Codrington looked at him suspiciously.

"How many?"

"Forty, Sir."

"Forty? The other captains told me they had cleaned the place out!"

"We got lucky, Sir. A ship was condemned, and I signed on her crew." James had his fingers crossed behind his back. There had been a ship condemned as unseaworthy while they were there. But she only had a crew of five and he had swept up four of them.

"The luck of the father runs on in the son," Codrington muttered. "Well, that's all to the good. Do you have any influence over the captains of those ships of the Intelligence Service? You used to serve under your father I believe."

"I know them of course. What do you want me to do, Sir?"

"Ask them if they can spare some men. All the fifth rates are undermanned."

"I will go across and ask them." James looked out of the window and saw sails unfurling.

"Aah, Sir," he said and nodded in that direction.

"Dammit! They are making sail. Where are they going?"

"I have no idea, Sir," James said innocently.

**

The new men were all prime hands and settled in quickly. The ship's book showed that all the new men joined in Malta and were former merchant seamen. None cared about that as their Marty would see them right when they returned to England.

Codrington detailed the Talbot and Dartmouth to patrol the Gulf of Corinth. The two were more than enough to face any remnants of the

Ottoman Navy in that area. They sailed north and then turned east into the Gulf, the Dartmouth leading. As they approached the narrows at Patras they looked for any signs of Turkish or Egyptian ships. There were none and the Greek flag flew over the town. A solitary cannon fired a salute as they passed and both ships replied with well-measured salutes of their own. Once into the Gulf of Corinth they progressed at a leisurely pace east staying close to the north coast passing several towns until they reached the Bay of Itea. James knew that this is where Hastings had sunk nine ships with his steam ship armed with only four guns.

"Signal from the Dartmouth. Search bay."

"Signal. Acknowledge," James said. "Turn due north, let out reefs."

They accelerated into the turn and with the wind from two points off of their beam sailed into the bay. The Dartmouth stood by in case it needed to lend assistance.

"Lookouts, keep a sharp eye out for rocks. Bring us to quarters."

The bay narrowed to the town of Itea behind which the bay continued. The Turkish flag flew over the town and there were a pair of ships in the harbour. Both had bare masts and were in no way ready for sea. James felt his way past the town, turbaned soldiers watched him pass but made no aggressive moves.

Once past the town they wore ship to reverse course and leave the bay. As they passed the middle of the town a Greek flag was waved by a person on a roof. James smiled, the Greeks still had fight in them.

**

Re-joining the Dartmouth, they continued east when a confused signal mid reported, "Dartmouth is signalling – smoke to the east."

James nodded; he had a strong suspicion they were about to meet the most effective ship in the Greek navy.

He was right the smoke resolved itself into the Kartèria. The three ships hove to and the captains gathered on the Kartèria.

"Captain Frank Hastings, Hellenic Navy."

"Captains, Fellows and Stockley."

Introductions made, they looked around the ship.

"So, this is the beast of the Hellenic Navy," Fellows said.

Hastings laughed.

"Let me show you around."

As they walked along the deck to where the massive guns were positioned Hastings asked James, "Are you related to Admiral Stockley?"

"He is my father."

"He is a great man and done much for the cause of Greek independence. Please pass our thanks to him when you see him again."

Fellows stopped by a sixty-four pound long.

"How many men do you need to handle these monsters?"

Hastings patted it fondly.

"Three teams of twelve and we fire explosive shot. The effect is quite devastating, you know."

James looked at a construction of bricks on the centreline.

"Hot shot as well?"

"Yes, the ovens are specially constructed so we can heat shot on deck."

That was something James would not want on a wooden ship.

Fellows looked thoughtful.

"How often do you change teams?"

"Every twenty minutes for these and the carronades. The shot is exceptionally heavy."

James thought about that. The carronades would fire a shot every thirty seconds or so with a well-schooled crew, the longs probably one every minute and a half to two minutes. The engine would keep the ship moving even with the wind flattened making her hard to hit. Explosive shot, handled well, would be devastating to a wooden hull.

"How do you time the fuses on your shot?" he asked.

"We spent a lot of time practising and calibrating the lengths of fuse for particular ranges." He went to a cupboard built at the base of the mainmast and removed a board. On it was drawn a table with the heading "64 LONG" at the top.

"The range is given to them by the gunnery officer. The loaders then refer to this and cut the fuse to the correct length. There is a separate one for the carronades."

James nodded. It sounded like Hastings had everything worked out.

"We sometimes have a shell explode after it has penetrated a hull. That is particularly effective."

"I'm glad we are on the same side," Fellows said, imagining the effect on his ship.

They visited the engines next.

"Each wheel is powered by its own engine which makes the ships very manoeuvrable. We can make seven knots under steam and spin her around in her own length if need be. The only problem is, in extremely rough weather the paddles come out of the water, especially if we have used a lot of coal and the hull is high in the water."

James nodded he could understand that but thought there must be a mechanical way around it.

Tour completed they retired to his cabin and had lunch.

**

James couldn't get the idea of fighting a steam ship out of his head. He imagined one with the carronades mounted on pivots like the Unicorn and sketched a design based on that. Then he thought, why not mount a long, on a pivot?

Laughing he abandoned that idea as impractical and probably foolhardy. His steward stuck his head around the pantry door and asked, "Did you call, Sir?"

"No, but can you make me some tea?"

"Aye, Sir."

He put away his paper and turned his attention to the daily grind of paperwork. Reports of the usage of stores, the health of the men, what they did and where they did it, weather conditions and everything else that pertained to the daily life of the ship.

He picked up a report from the carpenter, one of the planks that had been installed in Malta had not been caulked properly and was seeping water. They would have to fix that once they stopped at a port. He noted it, knowing that nothing would be done about it in Malta. Shipyards ran on bribes and there was nothing he could do about that. Other than that, his was a happy and efficient ship.

They stopped at Corinth to reprovision with fresh fruit and vegetables and James took the opportunity to heel the Talbot over and re-caulk the offending timber. As it was just below the waterline this was achieved by shifting all the guns to the port side then using a kedge attached to the capstan to increase the heel until the plank was clear of the water.

Men on bosun's chairs went over the side and hammered in the caulk before sealing the seam with tar. It was dry for the most part, but it was the rainy season and the men got wet occasionally. However, they were not cold as it was sixty Fahrenheit which, compared to England where it was thirty and freezing, was positively balmy.

Repairs completed, they ran back up the Gulf against the prevailing wind, making long tacks. James again imagined how Hastings would fare. Would he be able to use his engines in this sea? It was quite rough. Would he resort to sails or just anchor in a sheltered spot and wait for calmer weather?

Sailing a Desk

Marty chaffed, he had been sat behind a desk for a month now and he was, he had to admit, suffering from cabin fever. He would rather be on blockade duty than this. He sat back and sighed, he had read every personnel file and knew what operations were going on around the world. He looked out of the window which overlooked St James's Park. It was a fine and frosty morning. A clock struck twelve. He stood and rang the bell for his secretary, Adam entered the room.

"I am going for a walk in the park."

"Very good, Milord, how long will you be?"

"No more than an hour, I need some fresh air."

He pulled on his coat, scarf, hat and gloves; he was in civilian dress, and took up a silver-topped cane. It contained an eighteen-inch razor sharp blade and replaced the sword he would have worn if in uniform.

He got to the main door on King Charles Street and was greeted by a familiar voice.

"Trying to escape, eh?"

"Hello, Arthur, just getting some air," he replied as the Duke of Wellington fell into step beside him.

"Good, I was beginning to think you liked being in that office."

They walked to the park and adjusted their speed to keep them away from other walkers.

"Caught up with all the reports?" Arthur asked.

"Yes, I have read all the personnel files and assignments and am up to date on the reports."

"Excellent, you will be able to provide a summary to the PM and foreign secretary then."

"When?"

"Tomorrow at two, his office."

"Is that to be a regular thing?"

"Weekly from now on, along with an assessment on potential issues of concern."

"I will add it to my diary."

"What do you think about the Russians?"

"They are going to declare war on Turkey who have closed the Dardanelles to them and are expected to revoke the Akkerman Convention. Probably in the next year. We have two agents in the Russian court at the moment keeping an eye on things."

"As long as they confine themselves to the north, we will stay out of it. You need to keep an eye on it all the same."

"I will. The French are brewing up again internally. Charles is not a popular monarch and there is a growing faction that would prefer the house of Orléans."

"Hmm, keep an eye on that as well. How is South America?"

"A mess. Chaton and Lancelot are there now and installing themselves close to Bolivar. We can expect that area to bubble away for quite some time."

"I want you to disrupt Egypt. They lost ships at Navarino but still have an adequate fleet. Do something that will drive a wedge between them and the Turks."

**

Marty returned to his office feeling refreshed and realising that Arthur had given him the last month to settle in. Now the real work would start.

He looked at the Egypt file and saw they had just one agent there. That was not enough for what he had in mind. He wrote a message for Songbird to recruit a couple more in the Alexandria region and to pay attention to who the envoys between Constantinople and Cairo were. He also wanted someone in Ibrahim's court and asked for her to find out who was for and against the Ottoman Empire.

He remembered a name from his reading of the agent's files and asked Adam to fetch it for him. He returned with the indistinct brown cardboard folder and placed it on Marty's desk along with a fresh cup of tea.

Marty read. Adrian Faulkner, code name Snipe, father a major in the Grenadier Guards, his mother an Austrian. Spoke Austrian German like a native, and had learned Arabic and French at the academy.

Interesting, the Austrians continue to support the Ottomans and are welcome in Constantinople and Alexandria, Marty thought.

He read on, checking Faulkner's skills and the notes made by his instructors and handlers. *Calm under pressure, able to think on his feet,* and most interesting a note from Linette, *good looking and fit. A perfect specimen to infiltrate through the women of a household or establishment.*

"Or court," Marty said out loud. He rang the bell for Adam.

"Send for Snipe to attend me at his earliest. I believe he is in Ireland at the moment."

"Yes, Milord. Lord Hardcastle sent a note asking if you would have lunch at the club with him tomorrow."

Marty looked at his watch, it was already getting on towards five o'clock and he had promised to take Caroline to the theatre to see a new comedy play by James Kenney.

"The old duffer probably wants me to kill someone for him," Marty joked. "Tell him I will meet him at one."

**

The play was at the Theatre Royal in Drury Lane. It had a cast of worthy actors and was set in Paris. It was funny and entertaining, and they watched from a box with a bottle of champagne between them. After the show they had dinner at the Prince of Wales, a new establishment that had a separate room for dining. A new trend in London.

The next morning Marty was back in the office at eight. Adam, who had a rented house in Bruton Street for his family, accompanied him. They walked most days as it was just a thirty-minute stroll from Mayfair. As they walked Marty asked after Mima and his daughter.

"They are well. Susan is growing fast and already has all the womanly wiles to try and get her own way."

Susan was a beautiful child with her mother's delicate Burmese features tempered with a touch of English beauty. She was coming up to two years old and precocious.

Marty knew that Adam desperately wanted a son and the couple were trying for a second child. He was too discreet to ask, Adam would tell him if Mima fell again.

A letter was waiting for him at the office.

My dear father,

You are probably wondering why I sent this to your office not home. Well, it has to do with the navy and their lordship's refusal to contemplate steam power as a viable means of propulsion. I have had the pleasure and great fortune to have a look around the Hellenic navy's ship Kartèria captained by Frank Hastings. She is a sloop and has steam power as well as sails. She was built in Rotherhithe by Daniel Brent. She sails mainly under wind power using the engines during combat. Hastings was showing off her capabilities when he approached us.

They approached us sailing directly into the wind at around six knots under steam with not a shred of sail set. She is armed with just eight guns: four longs and four carronades, all sixty-fours. They fire exploding or heated shot and have worked out an easy-to-follow system for setting the fuses.

Their manoeuvrability and the exploding shot explains how they were able to sink nine ships at Itea while taking little damage themselves.

I tell you all this in the hope you may have some influence over their lordships, even in a small way.

I am very well, the sailing is good and there is very little sign of Ottoman or Egyptian ships,

Your loving son, James

Marty smiled to himself. He had heard what Hastings had achieved and knew that the navy powers were ignoring it. He chuckled at the sudden idea that Drake would probably be just at home on a modern ship as he was on the Hind. He had an idea, but it would take some time to put it into operation.

**

A week passed and Snipe finally arrived from Dublin. Marty greeted him in his office. He had obviously travelled fast.

"Did you arrive in London today?" Marty asked.

"An hour ago, Sir."

"Where are you staying?"

"At my parent's house in Kingston upon Thames."

All this time Marty was assessing the young man. Linette had been right, he was good looking in a chiselled, manly way. Fair haired, blue eyed, broad shouldered.

"Excellent. I have a job for you. Have you been to the Middle East before?"

"No, Sir. But I do speak Arabic."

"I know, and that is one of the reasons I have chosen you for this mission. You are to pose as an Austrian and infiltrate the court of Ibrahim Pasha in Alexandria."

Snipe looked surprised then pleased and just as quickly schooled his face to neutrality.

"I want to know what their relations with the Ottomans are like and what they are planning to do next. If you cannot get into the inner circle, then find someone who is and use them. Women are present everywhere in their palaces and are largely treated as being invisible. They hear everything. My suggestion is that if you cannot get direct access, find one and seduce her."

That was pretty blunt, but Snipe just nodded.

"When do I leave?"

"Your identity and papers are being created by the back office. After they are satisfied you have your cover story in place you will sail to Trieste and from there to Alexandria. You should be ready in a week."

**

That done, Marty took a trip down to the docks. There he watched the busy little steam tugs running around and manoeuvring the huge East Indiamen around with apparent ease. The little paddle steamers fussed, pushed and pulled, smoke chuffing from their funnels. One pulled over to the dock and the crew ran out a trough to a waiting cart. Coal was soon running down the trough into the tug's coal bunker.

"Do you need to take on water as well?" Marty called to the skipper who was watching from his wheelhouse.

"Naa, mate, she pulls what she needs straight from the river," he replied in a broad east end accent.

So you only need to load fuel and that can be coal or wood.

As the coal was loaded, he watched as the hull settled lower in the water. He was about to ask if that affected the efficiency of the paddles when one of the crew started turning a crank and the paddles rose up in relation to the hull.

"How old is she?"

"Straight off the chocks last week. Newest boat on the river."

"Do they all have that crank for the paddles?"

"Nope, only one so far," the skipper replied proudly.

That gave Marty food for thought.

He returned to his office. There were several ships in his inventory that were really past their best. The Endellion and Eagle were getting on now and should be replaced. If James was right in his assessment of the *Kartèria* then similar ships would be ideal replacements for the two schooners.

**

Marty had a meeting to attend on the growing Irish problem and had to put his thoughts of ships aside for the time being. Daniel O'Connell and the Catholic Church were campaigning for catholic emancipation at home in Ireland and in the broader United Kingdom. He had established the Catholic Association and campaigned for Irish self-government.

Marty had to find a replacement for Snipe and had chosen a female graduate of the academy, Blossom.

"She has Irish ancestry and is blessed with brown hair and blue eyes. We have created a back story and persona that will be attractive to O'Connell. She is intelligent, attractive and educated. Our aim is to get her into his inner circle," Marty reported.

"What about the Brotherhood?" Wellington asked, referring to the Irish Republican Brotherhood which was a more militant organisation that espoused the use of force to achieve independence.

"I was coming to that next. The IRB has already been infiltrated by the police, but they lack a man in the inner circle. We have a man, a former member of the Irish guards, code name Gunner, who has been in place for a year now. He has worked his way up the ranks in the IRB and is poised to enter the inner circle."

The Prime Minister, Fredrick Robinson, the home secretary, Henry Petty-Fitzmaurice and Arthur Wellesley all nodded, it appeared Marty had the problem in hand.

"I have a question," Marty said.

The PM nodded for him to ask.

"Why is my office in charge of this, not the domestic branch?"

"That is a good question," Wellington said. "We have an election in the new year, and everything may change, except your department. We need continuity on this."

Christmas

The SOF had returned to Chatham and Marty called Captains Ackermann, Archer and Trenchard to London. They arrived in time for Christmas. The flotilla was given shore leave while the Unicorn and Leonidas were being refitted. The Nymph and Neaera were being sold off and replaced by a pair of converted East Indiaman hulls that looked like merchantmen but were decidedly not.

"Gentlemen," Marty opened after greetings had been completed, "as you will have read in my communication the Endellion and Eagle are to be decommissioned and sold off. That does not mean you return to the regular navy or that the flotilla is in any way diminished."

The three looked hopeful.

"I have received permission to fund the construction of two new sloops to replace them along the lines of the Kartèria, Hasting's ship in Greece. There will be some significant differences though. Both ships will be commanded by captains."

Archer and Trenchard both broke out into beaming smiles.

"And they will be under the command of a rear admiral. Congratulations, gentlemen, on your promotions. Angus and Andrew are also making Captain."

Glasses of Madeira were served by Adam and a toast made to the newly promoted officers. Marty called them to order and continued.

"Now on to the new ships. The navy hierarchy is stuck in the last century and is extremely reluctant to move away from sail. We, however, are not constrained by them and can do what we like. The new ships will be powered by the latest steam engines available. These are more powerful than Hasting's and can run faster. For sailing, the paddlewheels can be lifted from the water to reduce drag, this also allows for them to be adjusted so that they work efficiently as the coal is used and the boat rises."

"How fast will they travel under sail and steam?" Trenchard asked.

"The shipbuilder claims they will do eight knots under steam and with all sail set and a favourable wind they should be able to maintain eleven or twelve under sail."

"What armament?" Trevor Archer asked.

"Two sixty-four-pound carronades mounted on the foredeck like the Unicorn, four fifty-four hundredweight, eight-inch canons firing exploding shot, two to a side and a further four thirty-two-pound carronades on the quarterdeck."

"Pfft they pack a punch then," Wolfgang said.

"Yes, and the engines will be different to the Kartèria, more reliable and more efficient, as I said before. They are a Woolf designed and built by Harvey and Company of Hayle so are the best available. The ships will be ready in four months as they already have two keels laid on the stocks. Now please go and join your families for the festive season and relax."

**

Wolfgang would, of course, be joining his wife Mary in the Stockley house in Grosvenor Square. Marty liked the idea of being home for the festive season and other holidays and the two of them and Edwin, who was on leave from the Royal Horse Guards, went into the city to shop for presents.

Wolfgang was quite wealthy in his own right from the prize money he had accumulated over the years and Marty suspected that he and Mary would set up house now he was an admiral. He could easily afford to buy a house in London and as Mary was more a friend now than a member of staff, they would always be welcome. That was confirmed when they visited Coutts bank to withdraw some funds and Wolfgang had a word with the manager about houses in Mayfair or St James.

Edwin, a lieutenant, had a number of girls he dallied with, but no one had won his heart yet. Marty secretly thought he was looking for a girl who could be compared to his twin sister, Constance, as all of them were blonde or strawberry blonde and taller than average.

Marty visited Wilkinson's while the other two went to sort out a new uniform for Wolfgang. He wanted to buy his two martial sons new dress swords. Edwin would get an 1814 pattern Household Cavalry dress sword. A straight, double-fullered, thirty-four-and-a-half-inch-long blade engraved with the regiment's battle honours. It had an ornate brass knuckle guard with the lion rampant on a crown and twisted wire embellishments.

For James he chose a sword with a twenty-nine inch slightly curved blade with a round back and double-edged spear point, the hilt had a lion's-head pommel, solid half basket guard with raised bars and a crown and anchor badge. The hand grip was wrapped in white fish skin and bound with gilt wires.

He joined the two at Graves and Hawks in Saville Row. Wolfgang had finished being measured and was chatting with Edwin as they waited for Marty.

"All done?" Marty asked as he joined.

"He is just finding out what it costs to be an admiral," Edwin joshed. Marty noticed he was acquiring a typically army sense of humour.

"Let's go and find something for our ladies."

"More weapons?" Wolfgang smiled.

Marty chuckled.

"Let's not encourage them any more than we need to."

They visited several stores until Marty found a sterling silver vanity set in a handsome wooden case veneered in coromandel wood, inlaid with brass edging and inlay. Inside it was lined in red velvet and contained a number of silver-mounted cut-crystal bottles and a set of sterling silver brushes, a manicure set and sewing accessories. He asked that they engrave Caroline's initials on the silver bottle tops and brushes and place a silver cartouche with the family crest in the lid.

For Constance, Marty chose a leather-bound copy of John Adams' *An Analysis of Horsemanship* in three volumes. For Beth he bought Charles Waterton's *Wanderings in South America, The North-West of the United States, and the Antilles in the year 1812, 1826, 1829 & 1824.*

That left Melissa and Sebastian. For Sebastian he looked for something novel.

"Gold-plated knuckle dusters?" Edwin suggested.

Marty rolled his eyes then had an idea. He led the others to a specialist shop he knew in Cork Street. The window display showed cutlery, folding knives and gardening knives. Wolfgang and Edwin looked at each other in puzzlement as Marty opened the door, which rang a bell, and stepped into the dim interior.

A small man, with a slight stoop, appeared from the back of the shop. When he saw Marty he smiled and without a word beckoned him to follow. He pressed a hidden button on a display cabinet which swung aside to reveal a doorway. The man entered and turned up the gas light. After Edwin and Wolfgang entered he swung the cabinet to close the door. The room was lined with weapons of every description and the burglar's tools of the trade.

"Milord, what can I do for you today?"

"Mr Grimes, I am looking for a present for my son-in-law. He is in the same business."

"Something concealed?"

"That would be ideal."

Edwin was looking at a rack of stilettoes and picked one up to test the point. It drew blood.

Grimes took it from him and put it back on the rack. "Don't play with them, son."

He went to a drawer and rummaged around for a moment before pulling out a riding crop. It was leather with plaited hand grip with a loop and a kite-shaped paddle on the end. It was stiff so probably had a wooden core. Marty grinned when he was handed it and gave the handle a twist while holding the body. He pulled forth a ten-inch triangular stiletto with a needle point.

"That will do nicely."

Wolfgang was looking at a display of knuckle dusters. There were plain ones, spiked ones, some with blades and one with a pistol built in. He chose a set of brass ones and hefted it, liking the feel. He slipped them on his left hand and drew a knife with his right. The combination felt right, and he felt that he could replace the knife with a short sword for a boarding action.

"I'll take these."

Edwin rolled his eyes. Such a weapon would never be allowed in the Guards, but something did catch his eye. It was a leather wrist cuff that laced up.

"What is this?"

"Aah, Sir, that is a very useful item. May I?"

Grimes slipped the cuff onto Edwin's left wrist and tightened the lacings until they were snug but not too tight.

"Comfortable, Sir?"

Edwin nodded.

"Now hold this lace here in your right hand and pull."

Edwin did and a long thin wire of sprung steel extended from the cuff. The last six inches were rounded and blunt so you could hold it without cutting your hand.

"You can take someone's head off with that." Grimes smiled professionally.

"I'll take it."

The wire wound back into the cuff under spring pressure.

"Is that a present or for you?" Marty asked.

Edwin looked slightly embarrassed.

"It is for me."

Marty laughed and patted him on the back.

**

Christmas came and Constance came home. Presents were distributed. Beth and Sebastian had bought presents before they left for Columbia and left them with the butler. Marty got *Don Juan* by Lord Byron; a somewhat risqué volume.

Wolfgang surprised Mary by presenting her with the keys of their new home in Curzon Street. She knew of it and had seen it but did not know he had bought it. The house was smaller than Marty and Caroline's with only three bedrooms, but it had been modernised in the last year and had running water, indoor toilets and bathrooms.

Snow was falling by lunchtime, and they all went for a walk in Hyde Park to work up an appetite. For once the snow was settling as there had been an uncommon frost that morning. The Serpentine had a thin layer of ice over it which did not put off a couple of very hardy souls who swam in it.

They were walking along Rotten Row when Edwin was greeted by a very attractive young lady of around eighteen years of age who was around five feet six with blonde hair arranged fashionably and even though she wore a long coat, one could see she had a lovely figure.

"Hello, Edwin," she said, blue eyes sparkling.

"Aah, hello, Anna." Edwin stumbled over the words as he introduced her to Marty and Caroline then finally to Constance. She was Anna Montague, the sister of one of his fellow officers who he had met (more than) a couple of times at regimental balls.

"So, you are his twin," Anna said, looking Constance over. "Mother says to be wary of twin sisters if you were to marry their brother."

Edwin choked and Marty had to turn away and examine a tree to hide his mirth.

"Oh, you have nothing to fear from me," Constance said grinning like the cat who caught the canary. "In fact, I would welcome a sister-in-law who knows her own mind."

"He hasn't asked me yet," Anna said in a sotto voice obviously teasing the poor boy.

"Why not?" Constance turned to him, joining in wholeheartedly. "Why haven't you asked her yet?"

"I, well um, err," Edwin stuttered going pink.

At that point his mother joined in.

"You must come to tea, we really ought to get to know each other better."

Edwin stood behind Anna shaking his head, eyes wide. His mother was relentless.

"Shall we say Thursday at three?"

He deflated with a look of resignation as Constance and Anna walked arm in arm like old friends.

Marty walked beside him.

"She is very pretty, and obviously has a keen wit."

Edwin ground his teeth.

"I have no intention of getting married."

"I would avoid dancing with her then, she looks to have a strong will."

Edwin looked pained then confused.

"She is lovely, and I like her. She is a wonderful dancer and a good horsewoman. But…"

Marty could hear the girls discussing horses. They were getting on famously.

"She is, what, eighteen years old?"

"Yes, her birthday was in August. I bought her a corsage."

Marty raised an eyebrow; it sounded like the nails were going into the coffin one by one.

"Then you could have years of freedom yet. But, having said that, she may not give you that long. Think of Beth and Sebastian."

"You think she has set her sights on me?"

Marty put his hand on his son's shoulder.

"I see a very pretty girl who is blossoming into a beautiful woman who has wit and intelligence and who may have set her cap on a wastrel of an army officer. She will wait but I doubt she will let you escape."

**

Between Christmas and the new year Marty visited the Daniel Brent Shipyard. The keels he had seen had been lain down in anticipation of the Greeks ordering more ships. However, that had not happened, so Marty had been offered them. His ships differed from the Kartèria in their engines and guns and the design had to be changed to take that into account.

Samuel Brent, the latest in a long line of shipbuilders in the Brent family, met Marty in his office.

"Milord, I hope you had a good Christmas?"

Marty was not there for small talk.

"Excellent one, thank you, what do you have to show me?"

Brent unrolled a plan and weighted it down on the table.

"The new engines are slightly bigger than the Kartèria's so the boiler is set a little further back as a consequence. We have widened the ship by a foot at the main deck to make room but that doesn't affect it hydrodynamically as the widening is above the waterline. The cranks for raising and lowering the wheels are here and here." He indicated them on the plan. The extra space used by moving the boiler means that the aft two guns will have to be in the captain's cabin."

Marty did not think that was a problem as all navy captains lived with guns in their cabins. Instead, he focussed on the wheels.

"The wheels are covered to protect them from shot. How do they raise and lower?"

Brent pulled another detailed plan out and showed him.

"The cowlings are high enough that the wheels can be raised by two feet, which is enough to almost lift them from the water while sailing. This gear here can be disengaged to allow them to free wheel while under sail."

That was a definite improvement designed by Woolf himself.

"Excellent, when will they be ready to launch?"

"Six months if the engines arrive on time."

Brent took Marty out to the slipways where the two ships were being built. Carpenters were fashioning ribs which were being fitted to the keels once ready. You could already discern their lines.

A Change of Leadership

As soon as Christmas was over the incumbent Prime Minister indicated his intention to stand down leaving the way clear for Arthur Wellesley, Duke of Wellington, to succeed him.

Arthur was a popular choice with the masses being the man who beat Napoleon and a national hero. He did not, however, live at 10 Downing Street. He maintained it was too small and preferred to live at Apsley House which was an aristocratic town house in the neoclassical style designed by Robert Adam and often referred to as Number One, London.

Caroline left for Malta with Annabelle Shelby to attend the birth of their grandchild. Melissa was due sometime in the next month. The Pride would do the trip in record time.

In Ireland, O'Connell was agitating for the emancipation of the Catholics and was campaigning for election at the County Claire by election that would be held in July. The man had been challenged by Robert Peel, the then Chief Secretary for Ireland, to a duel in 1815. Peel had been enraged at O'Connell's repeated use of the name Orange Peel when referring to him. The insult implied he was good for nothing except championing Orangeism.

Marty had sent Blossom to infiltrate the catholic organisations and was receiving weekly reports.

"O'Connell is a pain in the rump but he is taking great pains to keep his nose clean. He is professional in his approach to campaigning and is building a very large following. It is my judgement that he will win by a large majority if not a landslide."

Marty reported to the cabinet.

"So, he is a political threat not a physical one." William Lamb, Chief First Secretary for Ireland said.

Arthur looked at Marty, eyebrows raised in question.

"He is indeed. He actively opposes the use of violence. Any physical threat comes from the Irish Republican Brotherhood who are quite militant. I have someone who is on the brink of entering the inner circle, but he is able to report that they are planning a campaign of assassination and bombings."

Arthur looked thoughtful.

"Any way we can speed things up?" Realising what he said, he added, "I mean the infiltration not the assassinations."

Marty gave him a wolf smile.

"There is, but I think it better the cabinet does not have any connection with it."

**

A week later Marty entered Ireland with a fake identity that said he was a door-to-door salesman. He made his way to Dublin and took rooms in a boarding house. It felt good to be active again. He was to meet Gunner in a park at the end of Sackville Street.

Marty sat on a bench reading a paper. Gunner arrived and sat at the other end eating a sandwich. They didn't speak. Gunner ate his sandwich and tossed the paper wrapper on the ground before leaving.

Minutes later Marty stood, folded his paper neatly, looked down at the litter, picked it up and threw it in a bin on his way out of the park.

Marty would not ask another man to do something he had not done himself and that night at one o'clock, the two met in the shadow of Dublin Castle. Again, nothing was said, and they made their way to a single-bedroomed house in Flunket Street. Marty worked the lock on the front door then cracked it open. It moved easily so he pushed it open all the way.

The two men entered and crept up the stairs. At the landing Marty paused before advancing to the bedroom door, testing each step before he put weight on it.

They entered the bedroom where David Walsh, member of the central committee of the Irish Brotherhood, slept soundly after several pints of Stout and a few whiskey chasers. Marty pulled on a pair of gloves then took a vial filled with a milky liquid from a pouch on his belt. It had a pipette in the lid which he used to drip several drops of the fluid into Walsh's mouth. Walsh swallowed and grunted.

They waited.

Suddenly Walsh convulsed and Marty clamped his hand down over his mouth while Gunner lay across his lower torso. The man struggled and puke came out of his nose.

When he stopped struggling, Marty moved his hand away from the dead man's mouth and puke dribbled out. He pushed down on his chest and stomach and more came out. Satisfied, he arranged the body how he wanted it to be found, took off the gloves and put them and the vial in a leather bag with a lead weight, closing it with a drawstring.

After checking the room carefully for any other accidental evidence, the two men left, locking the front door behind them. The bag containing the vial of concentrated lobelia and the gloves was dropped in the river.

Walsh's body was discovered three days later when his absence from a regular meeting led to his colleagues in the Brotherhood going to the house to find out why. The death certificate stated he had drowned on his own vomit after imbibing an excess of alcohol. Marty read the death notice in *The Dublin Gazette* over a full Irish breakfast. It was time to go back to London.

**

At the next meeting with the home secretary, Marty reported that their agent was now on the central committee of the Brotherhood and the intelligence they were receiving was of high quality and in good time.

He also reported that Russia was about to declare war on the Turks and that they were amassing one hundred thousand men under the command of Emperor Nicholas I near the border of the Danubian Principalities. The government blamed the action at Navarino for weakening the Turks to the point where the Russians could expand. It was an uncomfortable time for Marty.

Over dinner with Arthur, and his latest fancy, Marty complained. "I do not see how they can blame me for the Russians moving into Dobruja."

"Ignore them," Arthur advised. "Politics is ephemeral and, in any case, this has been brought on by the Turks themselves. If they had not blocked the Bosphorus to Russian ships this probably wouldn't have happened. Now they face losing territory to the Russians and having to open the Strait to them as well. You did what you had to. I will have my people spread the word that this was self-inflicted."

Arthur snorted a laugh.

"My friend, you have too many allies for any politician to take you on directly."

**

A letter arrived with the royal seal attached. It summoned Marty to an audience with the king. This was not the normal mode of invitation and smacked of trouble. However, he couldn't refuse it and prepared himself for the worst.

The king had effectively secluded himself in Windsor Castle for the past couple of years and as Marty's coach crossed the Thames at Eaton and approached up Castle Hill he could see the royal standard flying over the Round Tower. The coach clattered through the gate into the quadrangle. Guardsmen stood at their posts at the entrance and saluted as he entered. The coach had to circumnavigate the quadrangle to come to the covered entrance to the Royal Apartments.

He dismounted from the coach and an equerry came out to greet him.

"His Majesty awaits in his drawing room."

Marty knew the man by sight and asked, "How is he today?"

The man didn't look at him when he replied. "He has had his laudanum."

They entered the drawing room to find the king sprawled in an oversized chair. He was extremely fat and had gout in his right hand and arm.

"Your Majesty, Viscount Purbeck," the equerry announced.

The king stirred and opened his eyes. Marty saw they were almost completely clouded with cataracts.

"Martin is that you?"

"It is your Majesty."

"Dammit, man, step forward so I can see you."

Marty glanced at the equerry who indicated he should move closer. He had to get within a few feet before the squinting king smiled.

"I have missed you, Martin. You understand me, not like the rest of these fools."

The king held out his hand and Marty could see the joints were swollen, Marty took it and held it. A chair was brought over and placed where he could sit.

"You asked me to come and see you."

"I did?"

The equerry stepped forward and spoke softly into his ear.

"The Greek question, your Majesty."

"Oh yes! Some idiot destroyed the Turkish Navy and now the Russians are invading."

"The Russians are angry that the Turks closed the Bosphorus to them."

The king looked confused.

"Why would they do that?"

"Because the Russians sent a squadron to Navarino."

"Aah, I see. Still, it was a damn poor thing to destroy their fleet."

"They fired the first shot, George."

The king screwed his face up as he fought the opium he had consumed.

"But weren't they provoked?"

"Some think so, but the reality is they ignored all attempts to talk and that led to the conflict."

The king suddenly changed the subject.

"How is my goddaughter?"

"Happily married and in South America with her husband."

"Doing some spying no doubt." George chuckled, his jowls wobbling.

"Sebastian is an attaché to the ambassador."

"Aah," George said and snored as he fell asleep, quite exhausted by the effort.

Marty stood after patting his hand.

"How much laudanum is he taking?"

"One hundred drops a day, Sir."

That was a vast amount. Ships' surgeons only administered twenty before an amputation. Marty sighed and rubbed the bridge of his nose. In his opinion his friend had only a short time left to live.

On his way out he was stopped by George's brother William who was the heir apparent and King of Hanover.

"Lord Martin! A moment of your time please."

William was currently the heir apparent because his older brother Frederick had died the year before. Canning had appointed William Lord High Admiral just before he had died. He was sixty-two years old and the only one of the three brothers who had remained fit.

"Will you walk with me?"

William was known for taking long walks, Marty winced inwardly but nodded.

William led him out of the castle and down to the Long Walk. Before they set out Marty asked his driver to follow them. The prince set a moderate pace, Marty dropped into step with him.

"My brother is dying. The doctors tell me he has probably less than a year."

"Then you will become King," Marty said.

"Yes." William gave a large sigh. "God, I do not ask for this."

"The burden of duty falls heavily, but we all have to bear it."

"Indeed." William sounded resigned. "George tells me you are a good friend and a useful advisor."

"I do what I can and try to give honest impartial advice."

"Yes, that is what he values. Your neutrality in terms of politics is legendary."

Marty actually blushed.

"I wish I could say the same for my wife."

William chuckled. "She is legendary in her own right, a formidable woman."

He stopped and turned to Marty.

"I would value your advice and friendship as you have given George."

Marty held out his hand.

"You have it, Sir."

How could he refuse?

**

Caroline was upset by the news, when she received her next letter from Marty, of George's condition and wrote to him. He answered, asking her to visit. She noticed that his signature was put on the letter by a stamp.

She looked into the succession and saw that William was next and should be followed by one of his children. The problem there was that even though William had sired fifteen children only four were with his wife and therefore legitimate. The last of those had died in 1822. Therefore, the throne would normally fall to Prince Edward, William's younger brother, but he had died in the same year as his father George III. Given all that and the fact that his two older eldest brothers were doomed to die without legitimate issue (Frederick had died the year before) Edward's daughter Victoria, who was only nine years old, was next in line.

"You poor young thing." Caroline sighed. "Let's hope William survives to a ripe old age!"

She promised to visit George at Windsor when she got home.

Steam

Marty visited the shipyard regularly, that way it encouraged the builder to keep to schedule, and he could help solve any logistical problems. The engines were delivered by three barges along with the wheels, raising mechanism and drive shafts. Mr Woolf came with them.

Marty went to the yard to meet him.

"Mr Woolf, so pleased to meet you at last."

Woolf looked at Marty, somewhat confused as no one had warned him that anyone would be visiting.

"I am sorry, you have me at a disadvantage, you are?" he said with a broad Cornish accent.

At that point Brent arrived having been warned that the admiral had turned up.

"Admiral Stockley. My apologies. I did not know you were here. I see you have met Mr Woolf."

Marty smiled. "We have just met but not introduced."

Brent did the honours.

"Mr Woolf, may I introduce Admiral Stockley the owner of the ships."

Woolf shook his hand.

"Is that the same Stockley who owns those fast ships that trade with India and the Caribbean?"

"It is but these are not for my merchant fleet."

Woolf looked puzzled.

Marty did some quick thinking; he did not want to expose the Intelligence Service as the owner.

"I run a security service for hire by anyone with a valuable cargo that needs protection. These ships will be employed in that."

"Oh, I haven't heard of that."

"You won't, we keep it quiet, and I would appreciate your discretion. Now tell me about these engines."

Woolf, given the chance to talk about his work, was enthusiastic and gave Marty a tour of the engine that had just been unloaded.

"I patented my original design for a compound engine in '04 and this is an improved version of that. Trevithick had the right idea with his high-pressure engine, and we have incorporated that into the latest design. You see it has two cylinders, the first is a high-pressure expansion cylinder and the second is a condensing cylinder as per the old Watt design. That way we get the best of both."

"And is it reliable?"

"It's used in the mines for pumping water. We have tested it for many hours and if properly maintained, is reliable."

"My engineers will require training."

"I can provide men who can train them on the ship when they join it."

"Excellent! Now explain how these driveshafts work."

The two spent a happy hour chatting as the barges were unloaded until Marty had to return to his office for a meeting with an agent.

After the meeting, Marty contacted Archer and Trenchard. He wanted them to select men from their crews to be trained as steam engineers and stokers. Further, he wanted the engineers to go to the yard as soon as possible to learn what they could from the installation of the engines.

**

In the Gulf of Corinth, James was getting an object lesson in the use of steam. While patrolling they heard gunfire and headed as quickly as they could towards it. Hastings had been attacked by a pair of Turkish ships which had approached from astern and upwind of him thereby having the weather gauge. He had lured them in then gone to steam power and spun around to take them head on. They had been surprised but still confident they could take him on and win. That was up until he swung across the wind and gave them a taste of his big guns as he crossed their bows.

Spinning his ship around he manoeuvred behind them and raked their sterns. James watched through his telescope from the main gallant yard as the steamship literally ran rings around the two corvettes and shot them to pieces. He knew what the future held and it involved coal and water.

That evening after dinner he wrote to the admiralty volunteering to captain any trials with steam-powered ships and/or exploding ordnance. He heard a call from the lookout through the open skylight.

"Cutter approaching, flying dispatches aboard."

He put the letter down and went up on deck. The Dartmouth signalled for them to heave to. The cutter pulled up alongside the Dartmouth, a minute later a signal flew up.

"Our number and captain report aboard," the signal mid reported.

James went to go down to fetch his coat and hat, but his steward beat him to it and met him at the top of the steps. Dressed in his best he was rowed across. Once aboard he was shown down into Fellows's cabin. He was reading a letter.

"There you are, James; we are being relieved and can return to Malta for reprovisioning. You have a letter marked urgent with an interesting seal. He pushed it across his desk. It had the Stockley seal on it. Inside were two letters, one from Melissa and the other from his mother

He read the letter from Melissa who was in Malta. She had given birth to a baby boy; his mother and Annabelle had arrived in the nick of time and the birth, they said, was relatively easy. Melissa disagreed saying the six hours of labour were tough, but their son was healthy with a good set of lungs. As they had agreed he would be called Martin Seth Stockley.

"I am a father!" he exclaimed.

"I thought that would be the news!" Fellows cried and came to shake his hand. "What is it?"

"A boy! Martin Seth."

The midshipman who commanded the cutter was still there and shook his hand as well. James turned back to Fellows.

"When can we leave?"

Fellows laughed but could completely understand the young captain's impatience.

"When the Glasgow and Rose relieve us in two days. I will make sure we are at the mouth of the Gulf to meet them."

James returned to the Talbot and cried as he boarded,

"Splice the mainbrace! I am a father!"

The men cheered and the rum was brought up. An extra ration was always welcome and if there was a reason to celebrate, the men would take it with open hands.

James went below and read the rest of the letter. It said little and he frowned as that was not like his wife. He unfolded the letter from Caroline. It started by congratulating him on the birth and saying that she had written to his father to tell him, but then it continued.

I am sorry to say that Melissa is suffering from post-birth melancholy. This happens sometimes and in most cases Annabelle tells me the woman recovers and is quite normal. I shall stay here with her, if you can return, please make haste as she misses you terribly.

James frowned, melancholy was not a condition he knew anything about, but he trusted Annabelle.

**

Five days later the Talbot and Dartmouth dropped anchor in Valletta Harbour and James was taken ashore at a point that was closest to his house. He burst through the front door and was engulfed in Melissa's arms. She was sobbing and he held her tightly. Caroline came out of the drawing room and smiled. Melissa had not shown any reaction since the birth.

She cried for fifteen minutes and then slowly stopped. James realised she was exhausted and scooped her up in his arms and carried her into the drawing room.

"Put her on here," Annabelle said and indicated a chaise lounge.

James placed Melissa gently down and Annabelle placed a pillow under her head. Melissa smiled up at James and promptly fell asleep.

"She has not slept properly since three days after the birth," Annabelle said quietly. "I did not want to drug her as the baby needs her milk and I do not know if it would affect him."

The three retired to the dining room so he could meet the baby without disturbing her. Caroline brought little Martin down from the nursery and introduced them.

The baby was beautiful in James's eyes and he had the Stockley nose.

"Hello, my little man. I am your father."

The baby woke and gurgled as he looked at him. Then James smelt something quite horrible. Annabelle took the baby and went up to the nursery to change his nappy.

Melissa slept for a good while and instinctively woke when it was feeding time. Martin let the house know he was hungry and she got him to her breast.

"I have plenty of milk," she told James.

He couldn't help but agree as her breasts were bigger than they were before.

"Will they go back to, well, you know, normal?" he asked.

"When I stop feeding him, probably. Why? Do you prefer them like this?"

James blushed then realised she was teasing him.

"I love you whatever."

Melissa's feelings and state of mind improved with James around. She had felt alone even with Caroline and Annabelle there with her. That and the fear that James would be in combat again had brought her down. Now he was home safe, she felt better about life. However, he couldn't stay forever, just while the Talbot was being reprovisioned.

One thing he did on the advice of his mother was to find a nanny. Rose was English, forty-two years old, a former army wife (her husband had died of the flux), who had two grown-up children of her own. She was kind, patient and caring. With her in place, Caroline planned to return home.

Melissa got James alone.

"James, I want to go home with your mother."

James hid his surprise.

"You don't like it here?"

She shook her head.

"It's not that, I just feel so lonely when you are away here. The other wives are all so much older and have older children. My friends are all in London."

James understood and he also guessed that she missed the stimulation that working with his mother gave. He held her hands and looked her in the eyes.

"Go home. If you want, you can start looking for a house. Somewhere near my mother and father."

Caroline was not surprised when Melissa told her she was coming with her. The girl had gotten over her romantic ideas of following her husband around the world. The baby had seen to that.

Rose agreed to go with her. There was nothing to keep her in Malta and came from Kent originally where she still had some family. She, like Melissa, and James adored little Martin. On top of that was the prestige of being a nanny to a titled family. Her standard of living had gone up immeasurably.

**

Back in London the new Endellion was ready to swim. Her hull was complete and engines installed. Marty was there at the launch and naming along with all the flotilla captains. The Eagle would be ready to swim in a week or two. Now the Endellion would get her masts and rigging.

Some of the crew were ready to board, including the ones who had been designated for the engine room. The navy had no formal designation for them, so Marty and Woolf had to come up with some.

"The men who look after the boiler and fire are called stokers in the mines," Wolf said.

"That makes sense. What do you call the men who run and maintain the engines?"

"Engineers, they have more knowledge about the mechanics."

"The squadron has marines that are classified as engineers, and the men chosen are from that branch as they have mechanical engineering skills." So that was how Engineer and Stoker became the designation for the new ratings.

It took another three weeks to fully fit the Endellion out by which time the Eagle was sliding down the slipway.

Sea Trials

Philip Trenchard, Captain Royal Navy, stood on his quarterdeck. The smell of smoke drifted back to him from the stack forward of where he stood. The Endellion was a flat-decked ship so the quarterdeck was delineated by a brass strip that ran across the deck.
The ship had been towed out into the stream which was at the slack at high tide. Mr Woolf came and stood beside him.

"Slow ahead both," Philip said his fingers crossed behind his back.

Jonathan Williams, the first lieutenant, turned the engine telegraph's levers all the way forward then back to slow. Down in the engine room a repeater rang a bell and turned its pointer to slow ahead for both engines. The engineers opened valves and jiggled levers under the supervision of the builder's men. The wheels started to turn.

"Helm, two points to starboard," the pilot ordered as nervous as Philip.

As the ship gained forward momentum the rudder started to bite and her bow turned. Philip made a mental note of the time it took to do that.

The sound of the wheels turning was strange to men who were used to sail, but here they were sailing down the Thames against the slight easterly breeze. Philip went to the helm when they had some clear water and tried a turn one way then the other. He wanted to know how effective the rudder was.

"Pilot, you need to give the helm instructions a little earlier than normal at this speed."

"Thankee Ca'ain, I'll do that."

He kept the speed to under walking pace until the tide started to go out. Then they sped up as the river's flow increased. He noted how the wheels kept them moving at manoeuvring speed.

"Take us up to half ahead both."

They increased speed to about four knots land speed judging by how the world was passing by. A little over walking speed; a horse would trot faster but he was taking no chances with his new ship.

They had been towed to the powder dock to fill the magazine and only after that had they been able to fire the boiler. The single boiler provided steam for both engines and was one of Woolf's high-pressure models.

"The engines are purring like kittens!" Woolf proudly declared as they rounded Coldharbour turn. The next turn was at Swanscombe and was one that gave all sailing ships problems with a contrary wind as it turned almost north before turning south then east past Tilbury. The Endellion navigated the turn with ease. The topmen and the trimmers could sit back and relax and the men made the most of it.

**

With the final turn at Cliffe Pools safely negotiated, they increased speed to full ahead to exit the estuary.

"Six knots, Sir," Midshipman Rob Barker reported.

"Thank you, Mr Barker. Enter it into the log."

Out in the channel the wind was stronger but still from a point north of east.

"Raise the fore sail and mizzen."

When he could see the sails were pulling. "Stop engines, raise the wheels." And once the wheels were up. "Set the main."

Things didn't go without a hitch. The starboard wheel raising mechanism stuck and had to be freed and the engineer on the port engine started to raise the wheel before shutting the engine off and disconnecting the wheel. Luckily the engineer from the builders stopped him before any damage was done. But all that was incidental and to be expected on their first run.

The plan was to sail around to Lulworth Cove and practise with the engines and guns. The wind was perfect for that and they sailed along at a respectable ten knots which would get them to Lulworth in the morning.

**

Overnight the weather picked up and they soon found that the wheels would dip into the water as the ship pitched and rolled. This caused the wheels to turn as they were decoupled from the engines for just this reason. On Woolf's advice Philip ordered the men to stay clear of any moving parts. Although the Endellion was a seaworthy craft and actually didn't roll that much, Woolf and one of his engineers got sick.

So it was that the shelter of Lulworth Cove was gratefully received by some. The stokers got the boiler up to pressure and they went to the engines.

"Bring the ship to quarters, Mr Williams," Phillip ordered as soon as they were under steam power, he had his watch in his hand.

"Fourteen minutes. We need to do better than that!"

Philip had them steer across the bay with the wind a point off the port bow.

"Starboard guns, load with solid shot and runout."

That was smoother, a gun was a gun and the gun crews had worked together on the old Endellion.

"Give me two broadsides!"

The watch was still out and he saw that they were managing two broadsides in a little under two minutes.

"Hard to starboard. Stop the starboard wheel."

With the rudder full over, the port engine pushing and the starboard wheel providing drag, the Endellion spun around in not much more than her own length.

"Half ahead both. Starboard battery, load and run out. Two broadsides."

The men changed sides and soon the guns were roaring again.

"Better, a minute and fifty seconds." More manoeuvres followed including backing the ship.

Then there was a loud crack and the starboard wheel stopped turning when they reversed it to see how fast a turn they could make. They dropped the anchor.

The engineer came up on deck, face black.

"The layshaft bearing has broken and the shaft jammed."

"Can it be repaired?" Philip asked.

"We should be able to." Woolf headed down to the engine room.

Philip went to his cabin and wrote up his log and journal. He described in detail their manoeuvres and what was happening when the bearing gave way. Then he sat back, thought about it then wrote.

The danger is that if we have a mechanical failure in a fight we could end up at the mercy of our enemy. Tactics that enable the reversion to sail to get out of trouble should be followed. In any case avoiding placing extreme pressure on the engines should be avoided. I would not recommend reversing an engine while making way forward. Stopping it is preferable in almost all circumstances with only a reversal in an extreme emergency or at very slow speed.

There was a lot of hammering and banging and eventually it went quiet. Philip returned to the quarterdeck.

"Pleased to report, repairs have been made, Sir," the engineer announced.

"Do we have steam?"

"Aye Sir."

Philip turned to his first.

"Get us underway, Mr Williams."

They edged up to the anchor, the men turning the capstan by the strength of their backs, aided by the wheels moving them forward slowly.

Philip turned to Woolf. "Could you make the capstan steam powered as well?"

"The engine needed would be too heavy, I think. But I will look into it. Your men can lift a lot of weight and there are a lot of them. I estimate we would need at least a one horsepower engine and have to gear it down significantly."

"It doesn't need to work fast, slow and steady is what's needed. It can also work at a constant speed as we can control the pull with the tension on the cable."

Woolf nodded but privately thought that the engines would need to be developed a fair bit more before they could do this.

**

They left Lulworth under steam and turned east against the prevailing wind. Philip wanted to see how the wheel mechanisms worked as the coal was used up and they became lighter.

"Full ahead both."

The telegraph rang and the paddles churned. There was a three-foot sea running and the Endellion took it on the bow.

"Seven knots and a half fathom," Abe Selby, the second, reported.

Philip moved to stand beside the helmsman.

"Swing us two points to starboard."

The bow turned and the ship's movement turned from pitching to pitching and rolling at the same time. The wheels continued to bite. Philip went to the starboard rail and looked at the wheel on that side. He could see it churn the water more as the roll lifted it. With this sea it was coping but he estimated anything over a five-foot swell would see it out of the water. He went to the port side and it was the same.

He knew, because Woolf had explained it, that the engines had regulators that kept them running at whatever speed was set so he only had to worry about the effect that would have on the drive shafts.

"Bring us back into the wind."

Smoke poured out of the funnel and blew back along the deck, thankfully above where Philip was standing. Down in the boiler room the stokers had to keep the furnace fed. They carried fifty tons of coal and twenty cords of wood in the bunkers. That gave them enough fuel to run for ten days on coal and an extra two days on wood if they steamed during daylight hours only.

As the plan was to mainly use the engines strategically, emptying the bunkers wasn't realistic but getting them down to half full was. Philip changed the stokers' watches to a three-watch system of his own device.

	Day 1	Day 2	day 3
0400-0800	Team 1	Team 3	Team 2
O800-1200	Team 2	Team 1	Team 3
1200-1600	Team 3	Team 2	Team 1
1600-1800	Team 1	team 3	Team 2
1800-2000	Team 2	Team 1	team 3
2000-2200	team 3	Team 2	Team 1
2200-0000	Team 1	team 3	Team 2
0000-0400	Team 2	Team 1	Team 3

This was a fair system that didn't overstretch the men.

**

After five days of continuous steaming, they learnt two things. First, the engines were reliable enough. Second, the lifting gear for the wheels had only enough downward adjustment to cope with five days of steaming before they hit the stops. That led Philip to rethink things a little.

Why carry fifty tons of coal if we can only use half of it? An extra twenty-five tons of munitions would be far more useful. I shall suggest a reduction in the size of the coal bunkers with a corresponding increase in size of the shell store.

"Set a course for London. We shall return to the yard."

"Aye aye, skipper," Alexander Phillips, the master said.

They went to sails and tacked north up the channel to the Thames estuary, then used the engines, burning wood to keep the paddles in the water. When they got to Rotherhithe the Eagle was just finishing fitting out. Philip sent a message to Marty that they were back and that he needed to report.

**

The ships were modified in accordance with Woolf's and Philip's recommendations. and once the Eagle had completed her sea trials, they sailed down to Chatham where they joined the rest of the flotilla.

Portugal

Marty thought he was going to have a quiet day when a report from his agent in Rio de Janeiro landed on his desk. Up to then he had not really had to worry about Portugal. The throne had passed to the seven-year-old Maria II in 1826 when her father, Pedro IV, abdicated in her favour. Her aunt, Princess Isabel Maria was acting as regent, and Portugal was relatively calm. However, he had recently read another report from Lisbon that the church and the nobles were angry about the changes to the 1822 constitution put in place by Pedro to enable Maria to take the throne.

These changes created a system of government with a legislature consisting of an upper chamber of peers and clergy, and a lower chamber of one hundred and eleven elected deputies who were elected by the male, tax-paying, property owners. The throne was therefore occupied by a constitutional monarch, and this was anathema to the absolutist upper chamber. The rumblings of discontent were hardening into open opposition.

According to the report, her uncle Miguel, who Marty had come up against in his time in Lisbon, was reported to be preparing to return to Lisbon. The official reason was to declare his allegiance to the queen. Where Maria, under the guidance of Isabel, was a liberal, Miguel was anything but. Influenced by his mother he was an absolutist who believed that the king was the sole source of political power. He also believed that he, not Isabel, should be regent.

Miguel was quoted as saying that as his older brother Pedro IV had declared war on Portugal and become the sovereign of Brazil, which was now a foreign state since gaining independence, he therefore had no right to the throne. The logic his supporters in Lisbon followed was that as Pedro had no right, then Maria didn't either, therefore Miguel was King.

Putting the reports together Marty concluded that the traditionalist party would take the opportunity to put Miguel on the throne and revert the country to a pre-constitutional state.

Marty checked the date on the report. It was three weeks old and had come by fast packet. Marty figured that Miguel would be a couple of weeks behind as he was a notoriously bad sailor and would insist that the ship heave to every night. He penned a message to the British ambassador, Sir Fredrick Lamb, warning what was to come. That would be delivered by the Endellion which would leave Chatham as soon as possible and wait in Lisbon while the situation developed.

Then he went to see the foreign secretary, George Hamilton-Gordon, who had just taken over from John Ward.

"Lord Martin, what can I do for you?" Hamilton-Gordon said in his Scottish burr as Marty was shown into his office.

Knowing that Hamilton-Gordon was inexperienced Marty sat down and took him through the history.

"King John and his wife were estranged because he supported the liberalisation of Portugal, and she was an absolutist. Their younger son, Miguel, was heavily influenced by her. He and I had a run in or two when I was ambassador to Portugal. When his older brother inherited the throne but abdicated in favour of becoming Emperor of the now independent Brazil he saw his chance. He is now on his way to Portugal to take the throne for himself. So, you see we are faced with a usurper taking over the throne and reverting Portugal to an absolutist state, that will not be tolerated by the people. It can only result in war."

George listened with a dour expression then asked, "I understood that Miguel was affianced to Maria, wouldn't the marriage have made him King?"

"Not in this case. She is the legitimate heir, and he would be consort."

"I see. I think we need to talk to the Prime Minister."

Arthur met them at short notice as he understood it was urgent. He was, as usual, decisive.

"If Miguel usurps the throne, we will break off diplomatic relations with Portugal and recall the ambassador. I will then expect you to provide covert support for the return of Maria to power."

"Should we assassinate him?" Marty asked coldly.

"No, that would set a bad precedent, just support the liberals with whatever they need. Martin, go to Portugal and oversee this."

Marty was surprised, he had expected to be in the loop but not on site. But he knew Arthur would not be swayed so just bowed.

**

The Endellion was ordered to wait while Marty organised himself and his office for a temporary move to Lisbon. Adam would come with him, and the writer would redirect all the agents' reports to Chatham where the SOF would run a shuttle service. Not the most efficient way to run an Intelligence Service but needs must.

Caroline was as pragmatic as ever, though a little disappointed to lose her husband so soon after getting back from Malta. He told her it wouldn't take long as he was pretty sure Miguel would throw him out of the country as soon as he was crowned.

The following day he entered the dockyard and went to the wharf where the SOF was moored. He almost did not recognise it as the only original ships were the two frigates. The new ships, even though they carried the same names, were very different.

The Endellion was tied up next to the wharf, smoke drifting up from her funnel. Marty, Adam, their trunks and several boxes of files were brought aboard.

"Take her out." Marty ordered as soon as all were safely taken down to his cabin.

Captain Trenchard gave the orders. Marty watched and listened.

"Let go forward, starboard engine ahead, dead slow."

The wheel turned and the bow moved out from the wharf. It got to about ten degrees.

"Let go aft, slow ahead both."

The ship moved forward then turned under her rudder to leave the dock.

"That's a lot easier than towing or kedging," Marty said.

"There is always a tug on standby if anything goes wrong." Phillip smiled.

The trip down the Medway was equally simple. Navy ships did not need a pilot and they easily steered around the sandbars and other obstacles only having to give way to an errant sailboat once.

Out in the channel they stayed under steam to clear the Downs and the sea traffic then set sail to follow the coast west before turning south. Marty was pleased. The Endellion was a good sailor, and the crew were becoming proficient in sailing their new charge.

**

Six days later they were steaming up the Targus. The sight of a steam ship was unusual to say the least and a crowd soon formed on the dock. Marty and Adam went straight to the embassy. He was sure that spies for the traditionalists would report his presence almost immediately.

He reached the embassy, announced who he was and asked to see Sir Fredrick. The pompous clerk told him he would have to wait as Sir Frederick was having tea with his wife. Marty, who knew the layout of the embassy from his time there, walked past the ass and headed to the private apartments.

The clerk in a panic tried to restrain him, which was a mistake. He ended up on the floor gasping for breath. Marty continued to the door of the apartment and banged on it with the head of his cane before walking in.

Sir Frederick and his wife were sat at a low occasional table drinking tea and eating cake. Sir Frederick was in his shirtsleeves and jumped to his feet when Marty entered.

"Who the devil… Stockley? What are you doing here?"

"Sit down, Freddy. The situation here is about to change radically."

Marty gave Alexandrina, Fredrick's wife, a kiss on both cheeks and pulled up a chair. Unflappable and forever a Prussian, she called for an extra cup. Thirty years junior to Fredrick, theirs was a love match. Marty liked her, she was intelligent as well as damn pretty.

"What is going on?" Freddy asked.

Marty picked up his cup and sipped his tea.

"You know that Miguel is on his way back to Portugal?"

Freddy nodded.

"Yes, we heard he is to declare his allegiance to Maria."

"That could be just a cover story to get into the country. We believe he and the traditionalists will take the throne."

Freddy was aghast.

"Usurp the throne? The people will not stand for it!"

"With the church and aristocracy united behind him they will not be able to stop it."

Freddy considered the news for a moment or two.

"What does London want to do about it?"

"We will break off diplomatic relations and you will go home."

Freddy was aghast.

"That's it?"

"For you, yes," Marty said.

"We should start preparing the household," Alexandrina purred in her decidedly Prussian accent.

"I have a ship in the harbour and will place it at your disposal," Marty said.

"What about you?" Freddy asked.

"I will stay long enough to set up a support network for the constitutionalists. We want them to remove Miguel as that way the country will be seen to decide its own future."

"Will you take over the residence?"

"No, we will mothball it. Caroline's wine import business has an office here and I can use the apartments they own. Officially, I am here to oversee the expansion of the business. My visit here is to say hello to an old friend."

"By the way," Freddy said, "didn't Simmons tell you I was having tea with Alexandrina?"

"He did, and he tried to stop me when I walked past him."

Alexandrina giggled, she didn't like Simmons and could imagine what Marty would do to anyone who got in his way.

"Oh, I suppose I will have to pick him up then," Freddy joked.

"Oh, I wouldn't worry, he has probably gotten his breath back by now." Marty smiled over his teacup before taking another sip.

**

While Marty was away Adam was getting things organised. He visited the office of *The Stockley Import and Export Company* and located the apartments that Marty wanted to set up shop in. Then he had the crew take their luggage and all the boxes of documents to the building. The company owned a three-storey town house which had been divided into three apartments. The second floor would be their residence, the first the office and the ground floor the home of the marines that would guard the place until the rest of the Shadows arrived.

By the time Marty arrived Adam had the office fairly well organised. He sat in what would be the bedroom and Marty had his office in the living room. He had acquired a couple of desks from the office and re-arranged the rest of the furniture. He had the marines move the beds down to the ground floor along with the chaise lounge from the living room. The comfortable chairs would stay as would the low occasional table. The dining room would make an excellent meeting room.

"You have been busy," Marty observed when he entered the office. He had already made sure the marines were comfortable. The four all had beds and a place to prepare food. For them it was luxurious.

"We live upstairs. This is our working area," Adam said unnecessarily as Marty had already figured that out.

Marty refrained from a smart retort and went to his desk. He pulled out a sheet of paper and started writing. The letter was to the head of the second house of the government, Afonso Braga, a leatherworker from Porto.

"Adam, can you run over to the embassy and borrow their interpreter? I need this letter translated."

"Yes, Milord," Adam said and set off.

Marty had finished that letter and started another by the time he returned with the interpreter in tow.

"Sir Frederick said to tell you that he wants him back, but you can have him full time after he leaves."

Marty nodded.

"What is your name?"

"Carlos de Melo."

"Carlos, can you translate this into Portuguese please?"

The man scanned the letter. "It need work to make sense in our language but yes I can do it,"

Adam showed him into his office where there was a second small desk suitable for a writer. Carlos sat and began to work.

Marty's second letter warned Maria that she was going to be usurped by his brother and the traditionalists he advised that she be ready to leave at short notice.

**

Miguel returned and was immediately proclaimed King by his supporters who advocated that he return the country to absolutism. A month later he dissolved the Chamber of Deputies and the Chamber of Peers. The British government broke off diplomatic relations at that point and Freddy returned home on the Endellion.

A month later he summoned the traditional Cortes (the Cortes was an assembly of the estates of the clergy, nobility and bourgeoisie that dated back to medieval Portugal), to declare his ascension to absolute power. This reversion to medieval rule did not go down well with the people as Marty predicted. He had been busy establishing connections to the liberals and their military leaders. Thus, he was in Porto when the garrison there declared their loyalty to Emperor Pedro, Queen Maria, and the constitutional charter. Porto was the home of the progressives and was seen as being enlightened by many parts of the country.

"You know that this will attract retribution from the king," Marty told Afonso Braga, as he helped draft the letter. Afonso spoke English and welcomed the aid of the much more experienced man.

"We must challenge him," Afonso said. "He must not be able to establish a powerbase in the north."

Rebellion and Arrest

The letter started a rebellion that spread to other cities. Pedro suppressed them violently. Marty wrote to Wellington and the foreign secretary.

The situation in Portugal is becoming progressively worse. On the one hand the rebellion has spread from Porto to many other cities, on the other Miguel is using the army that is commanded by the aristocracy, to brutally suppress them. Thousands are being arrested and detained in atrocious conditions and hundreds more killed.

My assessment is that it will take a full-scale armed rebellion with a trained army to move him from power and that is not going to happen overnight. In the meantime, I will support taking the rebellion underground.

He received a letter by return.

My dear Martin,

You have another month to get the rebels organised then I want you back here as there are other problem areas you need to address. I am sending Bedivere to take over from you there, he speaks Portuguese fluently.

Arthur

Marty knew Bedivere, who had been recruited in Rio de Janeiro. He was a quarter English on his grandfather's side and would blend in perfectly. On Marty's desk was a report from Snipe, who had ingratiated himself with the Austrian ambassador to the Egyptian court and from that contact gained entry to the palace. A young servant girl in the palace had been seduced and was feeding him all the palace gossip. Marty grinned; Snipe was probably enjoying gathering that intelligence a lot. He had also identified, through talking to the ambassador, people in the palace who were against being part of the Ottoman Empire. He was cultivating one and would try and gain access to any organised opposition.

This was all good and Marty was satisfied that the Middle East was in good hands. Another report was not so good. Gunner reported that the Brotherhood had identified several police informants and assassinated them. A move was coming and the security around it had been tightened to the point where only he and two others knew where and when it would take place.

Damn, that means we cannot stop it without exposing him!

Gunner did say that it would involve an attack on the army on the date of the Apprentice Boys March in Derry, which was the 12th of

August. He added that to the list of things in his weekly report to Arthur.

Later that day he was walking through Lisbon to meet a contact when he was suddenly confronted with a troop of soldiers. The officer stood in front of him and stated quite emphatically, "Lord Stockley, you are under arrest."

Marty did not resist even though he had support in the form of Chin, Sam and Matai who were nearby. He gave them a covert signal not to interfere.

"On what charge?"

"Insurgency."

He was marched to an army barracks near the palace and searched, thoroughly. Disarmed, he was marched to the palace and sat in an anteroom surrounded by guards. The Duke of Cadaval, Nuno, entered, they were old friends and the duke had somewhat liberal views even though he was an aristocrat.

"Nuno, I'm so pleased to see you." Marty stood to shake his hand.

"You too, old friend. I hear you have been up to your old tricks."

"Really?" Marty replied innocently. "What on earth could you mean?"

Nuno grinned then sobered.

"The king is peeved with you, which in these days can be fatal."

**

Back at the house the Shadows were busy moving everything to the Eagle, which was moored to the dock. Standing orders said that if anything happened to Marty they were to get everything they could to the ship and burn the rest.

They put all the files in two carts and got them down to the docks before a lookout alerted them that there was a large troop of infantry heading their way. Adam had them grab his and Marty's trunks before he set the timer on the fuse of a firebomb.

The soldiers were banging on the door when it went off. Windows shattered and flame belched out of the first-floor windows. The soldiers retreated to a safe distance. Firefighters tried to put the fire out but they were too few and too late. The house burnt to the ground.

The Endellion set sail and went up to Porto. The Shadows melted into Lisbon and waited for their moment.

**

While all that was going on Marty waited. The guard was changed, and he waited some more. Then finally a summons came to see the king. He was escorted into the throne room by a six-man escort, where the king waited dressed in a black military coat with golden epaulettes, buttons and an array of honours.

Marty bowed deeply as he would to his own king, sweeping the floor with his hat.

"Your Majesty," he said.

"You are not welcome," the king spat angrily.

Marty went to reply but a gun butt hit him in the back of the knee sending him to the floor. He struggled to his knees and said nothing.

"You think you can come to my country and ferment rebellion? I know it was you who persuaded my father to sign that damned constitution. Now you are here to try and make us keep it. Well, you are dealing with me this time, my Lord!"

I think he holds a grudge!

"You will tell us the names of your contacts within the rebellion."

Marty remained silent for a long moment until he heard a soldier shift his weight.

"Now why would I do that?"

"Because we will beat it out of you before we execute you."

"And cause an international incident? You want the Royal Navy in the Tagus? The British Army on the peninsula again? I am a Peer of the Realm and personal friend of King George. He will not stand for the abuse of his subject."

"They will never know. Your body will be fed to the dogs."

At that moment the officer who had been at the house entered the throne room.

"Well?" Miguel barked.

"The house was burnt down, and the ship left port. There are no signs of his men anywhere.

"What do you mean burnt down?" Miguel almost screamed.

"It exploded into flames when we arrived."

Miguel spun on Marty.

"Did you do that?"

Marty shrugged and said, "I was in your custody, your Majesty."

Miguel retained his temper with a visible effort.

"Throw him in the dungeon."

**

The dungeon was designed to intimidate, but Marty was not impressed. He was locked in a cell that was ten feet to a side and fifteen high. He had a cot with a straw mattress, a bucket for the necessary and a simple wash stand. It was lit by an oil lamp that was hung from a chain from the peak of the vault. He sprawled on the cot and listened.

Guards moved up and down outside at irregular intervals. He tried timing them and soon concluded they were patrolling randomly. There was a small vent in the top of the vaulted ceiling that was open to the sky, showing that it was night time. No one came to extinguish the lamp.

This is an old tactic to deny the prisoner a sense of time, lucky they didn't remember that vent.

He was given water but no food and after five days was feeling weak, at random intervals someone would come in and question him.

"Who are the rebel leaders? Where are they located? How do they pass messages?" And so on. The questioning was amateurish and unstructured and he remained silent.

On the sixth night something came through the vent and was lowered to him on a thin silk cord. It was a package of bread and cheese wrapped in a piece of paper. The paper had a note on it.

We found N and he told us where you are. Be ready tomorrow.

Marty ate the paper along with some of the bread and cheese and felt strength return. He saved some for the morning and ate it for breakfast. He expected that any rescue attempt would take place during the night and was surprised when the door to his cell suddenly opened, and six guards filed in.

"You stand up," the officer barked.

Marty stood and moved into position between the guards who had formed up into two rows of three.

The officer barked the order to advance in Portuguese and the guards marched forward. Marty fell into step. The route was different to the one that brought him to his cell and he wondered where they were taking him. They eventually came to a large iron-banded wooden door at the end of a long, dank passage.

The door opened and light streamed in, blinding him. He was marched forward and as his eyes adjusted, he saw he was in something that looked like an old Roman amphitheatre. There was a wooden pole in front of the wall of what used to be the stage. It was bloody and the wall had musket ball pockmarks.

He realised it was an execution range for a firing squad. He looked around and realised he was too weak to take on six soldiers and an officer. But he was damned if he would go down without a fight and braced himself.

"Hello, boss," a familiar voice said.

He turned and looked up and there perched on the top row of seats were the Shadows. The soldiers fell out and wandered off, discarding their uniform coats and hats which were gathered up and stuffed into sacks. Adam walked down the steps to the arena floor.

"They are all rebels. We stole the uniforms, and they posed as an execution squad. Walked right through the palace and down to the dungeon where they fetched you out to bring here. There have been so many executions lately that they were ignored."

"What about written orders?" Marty asked.

"Nuno helped us forge them. Now we need to leave before someone realises they have been duped."

The route to freedom was simple; they had a fishing boat waiting which was owned by a rebel. They slipped aboard and were out to sea to rendezvous with the Endellion which was waiting three miles off the mouth of the Tagus.

**

"Take us to Porto," Marty ordered once they were aboard. The second thing he ordered was food. While he ate, he had Antton talk him through the rescue.

"We contacted Nuno and he found out where you were being held. The dungeons are in fact old cellars that extend beyond the walls of the palace. You can see the tops of their ceilings sticking up in the gardens. Each of them has a vent to let air in which is sealed with a grill to prevent rats getting in. The grill can be removed for cleaning. Once we found yours we were able to lower the food down."

"Who came up with the idea of the execution squad?"

"Nuno, he said that there was at least one squad a day moving through the kitchens and that no one would take any notice of another. We got the uniforms from the barracks laundry. Luckily the king likes his soldiers to be clean and smart."

"You chose locals to act as the soldiers. Why?"

"Our faces are plastered on handbills and posters all around the city. They are pretty close likenesses too, so we think Miguel has been planning this for a while and been watching the house."

Marty frowned, that made sense and fitted into Miguel's profile. He was a planner, something he learnt from his days in the army. Marty wondered if there was a way to use that against him. Maybe rush him into a reaction?

**

Porto arrived and they approached cautiously under the Danish flag. The guns were hidden, and the Endellion looked like a merchant ship albeit steam powered. The Fort of Saint John the Baptist at the mouth of the river Douro was not fooled and a gun warned them off. The shot landed close, and Marty immediately ordered them to stand off.

"Looks like they have circulated a description of the Endellion as well," Antton said.

"Yes, we need to come up with a plan."

They returned to London and Marty immediately reported to his superiors.

"The situation in Portugal is dire, the abolitionists are murdering the liberals and generals are killing generals. The queen mother is behind most of it and actively encourages the attacks. The liberal rebels have retreated into Spain, France and England in their thousands. The government is in exile with their families and supporters are in Galicia.

"What about the Azores? Are they not supporting the liberals?" George Hamilton-Gordon asked.

"The latest intelligence is that Madeira has been subjugated but Terceira is still in liberal hands. We have been asked to take liberal ministers and aristocrats who want to evacuate to move there."

He was given approval and started on an evacuation plan that would keep the British government out of it.

The Passing of a King

Marty received an urgent summons to Windsor Castle at the end of May. Full of dread he took a horse and rode post haste. He arrived and handed the steaming horse to a groom before rushing into the castle. He went to the Royal Apartments and found George in the company of the king's doctor, Sir Henry Halford and the Archdeacon of Saint George's Chapel. George was sat in a chair as he was too fat to lie down and breathe.

"Martin is that you?" the king gasped.

Marty had to hold back tears as he replied.

"Yes George, I am here."

"I want you to witness my will. Can you call a clerk for me?"

Marty called for the king's lawyer as there was always one in the household. He came with his clerk and set up to write what the king dictated. George started and he had obviously thought carefully on what he wanted. His dictation was precise and clear even though he was under the influence of laudanum. The will was extensive and comprehensive, leaving gifts to members of the household, and friends alike. Marty was not surprised when his children were mentioned and gifted generously. He and Caroline, however, were not.

At the end of the dictation the king was exhausted and fell asleep after asking Marty to stay. Fearing that he would pass away, Marty sent for Caroline.

"Is he sleeping?" she asked as soon as she arrived.

George gave a resounding snore and farted loudly.

Marty just raised an eyebrow as if to say, 'what do you think?".

The king stirred, maybe the scent of her perfume filtered through to his brain.

"Caroline?"

"Yes, Georgie, I am here."

"Good. Martin, I expect you are wondering why you two were not mentioned in my will?"

He didn't wait for an answer.

"I want you two to remember me alive. Everyone else leave the room."

When they were alone he gestured to a French cabinet in the corner of the room.

"Look in there."

Marty went over and opened the doors. Inside was a sword and a gold brooch with an enamel miniature of the king. This was surrounded by a ring of small diamonds inside a rose diamond and yellow gold wreath surrounded yet again by eight large diamonds interspersed with smaller diamonds. The whole was surmounted with a diamond crown.

"Bring both," George ordered.

Marty placed the sword on the king's lap and the pendant in his hand.

"Before I die, I am making you an earl. That is my legacy to you. I am also giving you this sword that once belonged to Napoleon."

Marty was shocked, the sword was beautiful. Silver gilt pommel and cross guard, the hilt ivory inlaid with enamel, gilt inlay over the ricasso and first four inches of the steel blade. The scabbard was wood overlain with mother of pearl and gilt. George chuckled.

"I have two, but they only know about one of them," he said, referring to the executors of his estate.

Then he turned to the brooch.

"This is for you, Caroline; it is supposed to only go to members of my family, but you have been like a sister to me. Take this and remember me."

George seemed to brace himself.

"Call my chamberlain."

The gifts were concealed, then Marty did as he was bid and soon the Duke of Ancaster arrived with all the regalia for the inauguration. Apparently, Wellington knew of and had approved the honour, so he was inaugurated then and there.

**

Marty wrote to James to inform him of his earldom and that he, James, was now entitled to be called Viscount Stockley. Caroline was now Countess and the rest of the children stayed as Right Honourable. The sword and brooch were placed in the family vault at Coutts.

It was a matter of weeks later on the fourteenth of June that Marty heard that the king had received the sacrament. He visited one more time before the king passed away on the twenty-sixth of June at three-fifteen in the morning. An autopsy revealed he had died from upper gastrointestinal bleeding from a ruptured blood vessel in his stomach. An orange-sized tumour was found on his bladder and his heart was enlarged, surrounded in fat, with calcified valves. It was a wonder he had lived for as long as he did.

While Wellington eulogised him in the House of Lords as a magnificent patron of the arts, the greatest man of our time with a great preponderance of good, *The Times* published quite a different view.

> "There never was an individual less regretted by his fellow-creatures than this deceased King. What eye has wept for him? What heart has heaved one throb of unmercenary sorrow? ... If he ever had a friend – a devoted friend in any rank of life – we protest that the name of him or her never reached us"

**

The funeral was held on the fifteenth of July. Guns were fired all day to mourn his passing. Windsor was bustling with people eager to attend and they approached St George's chapel in a rush to gain entrance. Marty was in the procession which set out at eight thirty accompanied by the king's band playing "The Dead March in Saul", William IV was chief mourner.

Dean of Windsor read the service to a background of chatter that was most disrespectful. It seemed that only a few genuinely mourned his passing, the rest were there for the spectacle. The coffin was eventually lowered into the passage leading to the royal vault during which his titles and honours were proclaimed. It ended with "God save King William the fourth!" and the royal anthem.

**

The coronation of William and Adelaide, his wife, was held on the eighth of September and broke with tradition. He and his wife travelled in the Coronation Coach with a cavalry escort to and from Westminster Abbey. Edwin had the honour of being a member of the scort. No consideration was given to the public who lined the streets between St James and the Abbey.

William disliked ritual and the traditional acts of girding the sword and armills were omitted. William dressed in his admiral's uniform with a robe over the top rather than the vestments George had worn. There was no banquet.

**

Marty liked William who was modest and disliked ceremony and extravagance. He wanted to know what was going on in the world and had a monthly briefing by Marty. The people liked him and he could be found walking unaccompanied around London and Brighton when he was there. He was approachable and likeable while also being conscientious.

Wellington commented, "I have done more business in ten minutes with him than in the equivalent number of days with his brother."

Marty could help but agree but he saw storm clouds on the horizon; the king and Wellington were at odds over the Representation of the People Act also known as the Reform Bill introduced by the Whigs which would change the electoral system. The king wanted it, but Wellington vehemently opposed it. The people also wanted it and started to riot during the summer and autumn.

Wellington was forced to resign at the end of November and a general election was held which the Whigs won by a landslide. The new Prime Minister was Charles Grey. He had no foreign secretary and left

Wellington in charge of the secret service although he did not fully trust him.

"How are you getting on with Grey?" Marty asked at one of their regular meetings.

"Poorly, he knows I will oppose that damn bill to my death and he wants to know about everything we are doing."

Marty knew Arthur hated being overseen.

"Tedious but no more than one should expect. You are political rivals after all."

Arthur muttered something illegible.

"Do we carry on as before with Portugal?"

"That is one thing we do agree on. Yes, we do."

Evacuation and Relocation

Andrew Stamp, Captain of the Nymphe led the small flotilla of ships into the port of Vigo estuary. Along with the Nymphe and Neaera were three large merchantmen fitted out as troop ships. Their destination was the Port of Cesantes which had a pier where they could embark the rebel refugees.

The Nymphe would be the first to go alongside, aided by her boats.

"It would be a lot easier if we had steam," Andrew grumbled, then bellowed, "Get that cable across!"

The men worked hard, and a cable was taken across to the pier where it was looped over a bollard. The other end was nipped to the capstan messenger which the men turned to pull them alongside.

The gangplank was run out and Andrew walked down onto the dock where a tall man in a frock coat waited.

"All's well that ends well," Andrew said.

"The end justifies the means," came the reply. "Bedivere, at your service."

"How many will we be taking?"

"Around two hundred, mainly ex-ministers and aristocrats who plan to set up a liberal government in exile. They are led by João Carlos Saldanha."

"Where are they now?" Andrew asked, looking at the peaceful town.

"Two miles away on the other side of those woods over there. If you will take the aristos and ministers, I will go and get them moving."

"I will come with you."

The two walked to the camp. It was squalid with few tents and many people sleeping in the open. They had at least dug latrines so there was little disease apart from malnutrition.

João Carlos met them. He had arrived the week before when Bedivere had informed him and his fellow politicians that the ships would arrive to take them to Terceira.

"Phillipe, is this the captain of our ship?"

"He is, may I present Captain Stamp, leader of the evacuation fleet."

"Sir, if you and the senior people here would go to the pier we will get you aboard my ship. Then we can get the rest of these poor souls boarded on the others."

"You have enough space for all of us?"

"We do, Sir, and food for all." Andrew smiled.

"Thank God!" João Carlos cried and turned to a group of men that had gathered behind him. He spoke in rapid Portuguese, and they scurried off to collect their belongings. Soon a column of people was leaving the camp and heading to the pier. Phillipe, as Bedivere was known locally, organised them so that a person who spoke English would be on every ship.

Andrew led the column to the pier where the Neaera had tied up alongside the Nymphe. Andrew asked João Carlos to bring his people aboard.

"We have room for forty aboard each of these ships. The merchantmen can take sixty each in comfort or more if necessary."

The elite families and their servants added up to forty-six for the Nymphe and forty-three for the Neaera. They were loaded quickly, and the ships towed out to make room for the merchantmen. The next hundred people were loaded in short order and the last sixty just before it got dark.

The sounds of singing rang around the estuary that evening as stomachs were filled for the first time in weeks. On the Nymphe, James entertained the most senior people over dinner with his officers.

"You are very well armed for a merchantman captain," João Carlos commented. He and his wife sat to Andrew's right and Stanley Hart, the first lieutenant to his left.

"The Nymphe and the Neaera are East Indiamen. We are normally on the China or India route which is rife with pirates. We need to defend our cargo and passengers," Andrew answered, keeping to their cover story.

"So how is it that such valuable ships have been diverted to help us?"

"You have friends in England, and they have funded the chartering of the ships." Also consistent with the story Bedivere had told.

"We are eternally grateful to them; do you know who they are?"

"They are a consortium of merchants who have lost their trade with Portugal because of the current situation, headed by Viscount Stockley and his wife."

This was true. The wine merchants who owned the trade in Port, Madeira and Dow wines were losing money because the exports from Portugal had slowed significantly as foreigners were being made unwelcome under Miguel, especially the British and French who refused to formally recognise him. The Americans, Spanish and the Vatican did and while Spain tolerated the presence of the refugees, they did nothing to help them. Lady Caroline had persuaded a group of traders to stump up some of the money to charter the ships and fit them out. The Intelligence Service had topped up the funds on behalf of the government.

The next morning more refugees were on the pier and boats were sent to take them aboard. At ten o'clock the tide started going out and the ships set sail.

**

The trip to the Azores was rough. Storms bedevilled them and the passengers were seasick. Terceira was thirteen hundred miles away and the ships could only make two hundred miles a day which meant seven days of misery for passengers and crew.

Andrew looked at Stanley Hart as yet more buckets of puke were tossed over the side. Stanley was looking over the side at something.

"Are we leaving a trail of puke?"

"We are, and the fish are loving it."

Andrew stepped to the rail on the port quarter he saw disturbance in the water and then several fish leapt into the air followed by a very large tuna.

"The predators gather," he muttered to himself."

A very pale João Carlos came to the foot of the steps to the quarterdeck.

"Permission to come up, Captain?"

"Granted. How are you feeling?" Andrew said cheerfully.

"Sick. Do you think this will continue?"

"Probably, I am afraid. It is the time of year."

João Carlos gulped as a wave of nausea hit him.

"I suppose you are used to it."

"One gets one's sea legs in time. Nelson was a very bad sailor and got sick all the time, you know."

"Really," João Carlos gulped and started moving to the windward side. Andrew grabbed him and steered him to the leeward side where he retched several times.

"Try watching the horizon. It helps," Andrew said.

For the next half an hour João Carlos stood with a death grip on a stay, eyes fixed to the horizon.

**

They approached Terceira Island and were immediately confronted by a British frigate which they identified as HMS Druid, a forty-six gun fifth-rate. The Druid approached and flew the query signal. Andrew ordered the Portuguese flag to be raised under the Red Ensign. That got her captain's attention and he closed to hailing distance.

"Ahoy there, what is your destination and cargo?"

Andrew looked along the deck where most of the passengers were lining the rail.

"We are British merchantmen carrying refugees from Portugal to Terceira," he bellowed back through a speaking trumpet.

"Under whose authority?"

"Admiral Stockley and the government in exile!"

On the Druid, Captain Somerson looked at his first who shrugged.

"Stockley has taken over from Turner at the Foreign Office. Something to do with Intelligence."

Somerson frowned.

"Hmm, I have a vague recollection he had something to do with Portugal before."

He took a telescope and scanned the side of the Nymph.

"Well dressed for refugees. We will escort them into Praia de Vitória."

Andrew accepted the escort and followed the Druid into the port. Once anchored João Carlos was boated ashore to talk to the local governor. James went across to the Druid where he was piped aboard.

"Captain Stamp of the Nymph."

"Andrew Stamp?" the first asked.

"Yes, that is me. Why do you ask?"

"Yours is an unusual name and I saw your promotion announced in *The Gazette*."

Captain Somerson sensed something was up and interjected.

"Let's go down to my cabin and discuss this in private."

He gave orders for the quarterdeck to be cleared so no one could listen through the skylight.

Now," he said as they sat in his cabin, "what is going on?"

Andrew pulled his commission and orders from his jacket pocket and handed them over.

"I am tasked with leading and protecting this fleet of merchantmen from the Portuguese Usurper's navy. We are transporting the Portuguese rebels and government in exile to sanctuary on the island."

Somerson looked sceptical.

"How can a pair of East Indiamen protect against an attack by warships?"

"We are armed with thirty-six twenty-four-pound longs, four sixty-four hundredweight ten pounders, two sixty-four-pound carronades on the fore deck, and six thirty-two-pound carronades on the quarterdeck. The ships are part of the Intelligence Service's Special Operations Flotilla."

The first, who introduced himself as David Wargrave, grinned.

"The infamous HMS Invisible."

Andrew grinned back. "Exactly."

Somerson was still digesting the strength of the Nymph and Neaera's armaments.

"How many men do you carry?"

"Three hundred."

"Good Lord!"

"I must caution you both that this conversation must not leave this cabin. It never happened. The government wants to be able to deny any involvement in this and as far as the world is concerned it was funded by and carried out by merchants with a vested interest in trade to Portugal."

Somerson handed Andrew's orders and commission back.

"Can I offer you a glass of Madeira?"

"Thank you, that would be wonderful."

As they drank Somerson looked out of his transom windows at the Neaera.

"Now that I look at her carefully, I can see that she has twice the gunports I first thought and those piles of deck cargo must be the carronades."

The side of the Neaera's gundeck had been painted with the Nelson pattern of black and yellow checkerboard.

"Yes, we only paint every other gunport yellow. Black is good for concealing the rest. You are correct in your assumption about the carronades."

Wargrave chuckled.

"Anybody who attacks you is going to get one hell of a surprise."

**

João Carlos returned with a civilian. He introduced him to Andrew.

"This is the governor of the island, Alvarez Del Porto."

Andrew dipped a bow.

"Pleased to meet you, Sir."

The governor spoke in rapid Portuguese. João Carlos translated.

"After Madeira was taken by Miguel's navy, they came here." He stood proudly, "We fought them off. They did not expect our coastal forts to be armed and strong."

Andrew had noticed the rough fortifications on the coast with their array of cannons as they came in. The guns looked old and mismatched but from what Del Porto was telling him, effective. He also had the passing thought that his explosive shells would reduce them to uselessness in no time.

The disembarkation of the refugees started soon after. Ships boats shuttled back and forth carrying people and whatever possessions they had managed to bring. The merchantmen also carried cargos of grain and rice which were unloaded to help the island cope with the sudden influx of mouths to feed.

Once free of passengers and cleaned up to Andrew's satisfaction, the Nymphe left the rest of the fleet in the Neaera's hands and set sail for Brazil. She had an appointment with an emperor.

**

Meanwhile the queen in exile arrived in London via Paris and was met by King William who summoned Marty to attend the two of them at Windsor. Marty arrived and was escorted by an equerry to the king's apartments. When he entered he found William in the company of two young girls.

"Martin, you are here at last."

As fast as I could!

"Your Majesty, I made all haste," he said and swept a courtiers bow to all three of them.

"Girls," William pronounced it *gals,* "this is Viscount Martin Stockley. Admiral who ruined the Ottoman's fleet and head of the overseas office of the Intelligence Service."

The girls curtsied daintily.

"Martin, it is my pleasure to introduce Queen Maria of Portugal and my niece Princess Alexandrina Victoria."

"My pleasure, ladies."

Maria looked at him and smiled. "I understand you have recently been in Portugal."

"I had the benefit of meeting your uncle. The cellars under the palace are most interesting."

Her hand went to her mouth.

"He imprisoned you?"

"For a short time. I was luckier than most and escaped with the help of some of your loyal subjects."

She looked very young when she asked, "Are my people suffering?"

Marty considered his answer and decided on the truth.

"Miguel and his mother are hunting down and imprisoning the liberals and ruthlessly quashing any rebellion. Those that can are fleeing to Spain, France and England. I have helped to get the members of the government who support you to Terceira where they have set up a government in exile. I have also sent word to your father."

"But your government supports Miguel!"

"Politics, your Majesty. The merchants have many seats in parliament, so Wellington has to appear to appease them."

Alexandina Victoria looked up.

"If I was Queen, I would not allow that," the ten-year-old said.

Marty knew that she would become Queen as the only one between her and the throne was William, so gently said, "Then your Highness would be at loggerheads with your government which would be unfortunate."

William laughed.

"My dear, my advice is to keep Lord Martin here close. His advice and that of his wife is always grounded in good common sense tempered with a canny knowledge of the world. He is also good at sorting out 'problems' that one doesn't want to become public. Talking of which, what can you do to help?"

"We will do what we can. It is best that you do not know what."

William noticed the use of 'we'.

"Send that lovely wife of yours my regards. How is your daughter?"

"Last I heard she is in fine fettle. Her husband is an attaché to the ambassador to the court of Simon Bolivar in Columbia."

"Up to no good then."

They sat and talked for an hour after which Marty excused himself. He was very impressed with both young ladies and resolved to do all he could to help them now and in the future.

Dom Pedro IV

The Nymphe pulled into Rio de Janeiro and Andrew Stamp went ashore as soon as they were anchored and made his way to the City Palace and seat of the Brazilian government. On his arrival he announced that he had urgent news of Emperor Pedro's daughter and the state of Portugal.

For once he had found a palace official with the gumption to send a messenger to the emperor telling him that a British ship had arrived with an urgent message. The messenger returned with a summons for Andrew to present himself to the court.

The emperor met him in an anteroom away from the prying ears in the main throne room.

"The message said you have urgent news about my daughter and Portugal."

"Yes, your Majesty, grave news. Your brother has usurped the throne of Portugal, and your daughter is in exile."

"Meu Deus. What has he done?"

"Miguel arrived and the aristocrats and Church almost immediately declared him the rightful king. They maintained that as you were Emperor of a hostile nation you were not entitled to the throne and by that logic neither was Maria. The absolutists then abandoned the constitutional charter and named him absolute monarch."

"The people will not stand for it!" Pedro proclaimed angrily.

"The people have no choice. Miguel is ruling with an iron fist and any signs of rebellion are violently quashed. Thousands have left

Portugal for Spain, France and Britain. I myself helped evacuate the liberal government to Terceira in the Azores where they plan to set up a government in exile."

This was the last thing Pedro wanted to hear. His relationship with the agricultural magnates, who held an enormous amount of power, was strained and his power base fragile.

"I thank you for bringing this news. I have some decisions to make."

**

Andrew was getting the Nymphe ready for the return trip when a messenger summoned him to the palace again. He was ushered into the same anteroom where he waited for the emperor. Pedro arrived dressed in much simpler clothes than before.

"I have abdicated my throne in favour of my son so I can go to Europe and help my daughter and country."

Andrew knew his son was barely five years old but could not question him. Pedro continued.

"I and a few trusted generals will sail to Britain to find my daughter then organise a counter rebellion. We have a ship, but can you escort us?"

Andrew agreed immediately as he understood that any ship sailing from Brazil would be subject to close scrutiny by any Miguelist ships that came across it. They would be less inclined if that ship was escorted by a British warship.

"When do we sail?"

"In one week, at the end of the month."

With no way to let Marty know Andrew hoped he had made the right decision.

The week went by really quickly as they took the time to service the engines. A week of shore food did not hurt the crew either. A pair of bullocks were added to the manger and a new goat for milk. Andrew discovered a liking for Jaboticaba jelly made from the fruit of the same name that grows directly on the trunk of a tree. A bushel or two of cashew nuts were stowed away along with a barrel of mangos. The surgeon stocked up on lime juice and Andrew got himself a couple of pineapples which were an absolute luxury in Britain.

Andrew also met a stunning Brazilian girl, her tanned skin, long brown hair and beautiful eyes entranced him. She was sweet natured and a good cook. A week was not long enough to form a permanent relationship, but his evenings were much more enjoyable than being alone.

They set sail on time which amazed Andrew as his experience so far of the Brazilians was that they were rather disorganised, but perhaps that was just an impression rather than actuality. The Nymphe followed the Barroso, out of harbour.

The journey north up through the Caribbean was regulation and they slaughtered one of the bullocks as they passed Jamaica. Roast beef for all the crew was a treat! They turned east to follow the trade winds off the mouth of the Delaware and make the Atlantic crossing. It was then that she was discovered. Consuella had come aboard to say farewell to Andrew but unbeknown to him never left. She had slipped down into the orlop deck and hidden in the surgeon's store room. With no way to get her back to Brazil he had to take her with him.

**

It was a big ocean and the last thing Andrew expected was to run into any Portuguese ships. He expected that there was a small chance that they may come across ships travelling from the Americas or Caribbean to Europe but even that was slight. So to see a ship flying the Portuguese flag coming up behind them was a surprise. She was gaining albeit slowly.

"It is a frigate," Filius Grantham, the second lieutenant, said quite unnecessarily.

The Barroso was signalling.

"Get us alongside within hailing distance." Andrew wanted no misinterpretation of signals.

"Ahoy the Barroso. We will confront and delay the frigate behind us. You must keep sailing and get to England!" Andrew bellowed through his trumpet.

**

On the Portuguese frigate, the captain watched the merchantman slow and drop behind the Barroso which was his target. She was an East Indiaman of the older, larger design. Probably sold off after the war when they changed to smaller hulls with less guns. He studied her and from what he could see she had only ten gunports to a side. She was flying the Brazilian flag.

"We will sail past her. Keep after the Barroso."

He watched, seeing a lot of activity on deck and suddenly there were carronades on her quarterdeck and foredeck. Then her gun ports opened.

"What in God's name!"

She sprouted twenty guns along her side. Sails bloomed and she matched their speed, stationing herself two cables off his starboard beam and slowly closing.

"Go to quarters!"

A plume of smoke erupted from the forward gun of the Indiaman followed by the bang. It sounded odd. Fifty yards ahead a shot exploded dead in line with them and about twenty feet above deck height.

"They are armed with exploding shot!" his first exclaimed.

It was a clear warning.

"Should we run out?" the first asked.

The captain scanned the barrels of the guns facing him. The fore-and-aft guns were different. Whereas the majority were twenty-four-pounders, those two were bigger. The carronades on the foredeck were massive sixty-eight-pounders, the ones on the quarterdeck thirty-twos.

"We are out gunned," he said in amazement.

Just then one of the thirty-two-pound carronades fired. He saw the bar shot shimmer in the air, then heard the howl as it flew overhead neatly taking the top of his mainmast off along with his pennant.

"Reduce sail."

"But Captain!"

"Do not be a fool. They can shred our rigging anytime they want. Their guns, as they have demonstrated, are loaded and ready to fire and they have exploding shells."

The ship which had no name on the stern escorted them until they turned south to home.

**

The Nymphe got into London two days after the Barroso. A messenger summoned Andrew to the admiral's office. When Andrew entered Marty greeted him.

"Glad to have you back, Andrew, now tell me about the Portuguese frigate and the girl you brought home."

Andrew had known that he couldn't hide anything from his admiral and passed Marty his report. Marty put it to one side and indicated he should continue. The report was delivered in the navy fashion, without embellishment and succinctly.

"You did not speak to the Portuguese at all?"

"No, Sir, we let our guns do the talking along with a few hand signals."

"Nothing crass I hope."

Andrew chuckled at the thought.

"No, Sir, just slow down and go that way."

"The damage to their ship was minimal and a show of force enough to persuade them that attacking the Brazilian ship was a bad idea. You did a good job."

"Thank you, Sir."

"Now, tell me about the girl."

**

Dom Pedro met with his daughter.

"Did Miguel hurt you?"

"No, Papa, but he has hurt my people, which is the same thing."

Pedro smiled. His daughter was young, but her heart and soul belonged to the Portuguese people. He looked into her eyes and reassured her.

"We will take back the throne and Miguel will be sent into exile."

"You will not execute him?"

"His mother is to blame; she has made him what he is. I will not kill my own family members. If she is still alive when we take it back, she will be exiled as well."

"What do we do now?" Maria asked.

"I plan a counter coup. There are thousands of exiles who will fight and many French and British who will fight for liberalism as well."

Maria looked at him with wide eyes.

"Will I be Queen again then?"

He cupped her chin with his hand.

"Yes, my little dove, you will be Queen again."

**

Things started to go wrong when Pedro met with Grey the new Prime Minister.

"I am sorry, Dom Pedro, we cannot allow you to recruit an army from the shores of Britain. The commercial relationship between Portugal and the British Empire is too valuable to endanger."

"What do you suggest I do then? I need to get that usurper off the throne!"

Grey dismissed the servant that was hovering in the room and told the clerk to summon Viscount Stockley then take a walk before saying quietly, "Privately I agree with your cause, but the merchants hold a lot of votes in parliament. If we try to allow anything that disrupts their trade which has already been damaged, we will be voted down."

There was a knock at the door and Marty walked in.

"That was damned quick, where were you?" Grey barked.

"In the cabinet room chatting to the foreign secretary." Marty smiled then bowed to Dom Pedro.

"Dom Pedro, I am pleased to meet you."

Grey introduced him.

"This is Viscount Stockley who is the head of the overseas branch of our Intelligence Service."

"How can I be of service?" Marty asked.

"Officially we cannot be seen to take sides right now in the dispute over the throne of Portugal," Grey said.

Marty held up his hand forestalling any more instructions.

"Understood, Dom Pedro, would you come with me?"

Grey gave a rare smile. Marty indeed understood the need for him to be able to deny any knowledge of what he was going to do.

**

Marty led Dom Pedro out of the back door of number 10 and into his personal carriage that was waiting for him. They talked as the carriage took them to Grosvenor Square.

"I knew your father quite well," Marty told him.

"He mentioned you. He said if ever I wanted advice, I should call on you. I never thought I would have to."

Marty grinned.

"You never know in this world what is going to happen. Look at the French. Just when we thought they had settled down, they go and have a second revolution and threw out the Bourbons and put the duke of Orléans on the throne."

"You approve of that?"

"I approve of constitutional monarchies. Charles was an absolutist and loathed by the people much like Miguel in Portugal."

"You influenced his overthrow?"

"Not at all, we monitored what was going on and had people in the right places, but the French love a good revolution and needed no prompting."

Pedro nodded. "Do you think the new French government will be sympathetic to my cause?"

"Undoubtedly, your cause is close to your hearts and if we can get them to take the lead in assisting you then Grey can tag along with the excuse that he is looking after British interests."

"You have obviously thought this through already."

"I have already been taking care of your interests."

Pedro's eyes widened.

"The fleet that took the people to Terceira!"

"And other things. I have had occasion to come up against Miguel and your mother in the past. If I may say so, she needs to be put somewhere she can do no harm."

Pedro agreed, his relationship with his mother had been distant. Miguel had been and still was her favourite.

"She and my father never saw eye to eye on anything. It is a wonder they ever had children."

Marty knew about their relationship having seen it first-hand.

"While their marriage was not based on love, they both had a strong sense of duty. Even while they were political opposites, they were the ruling couple, and their duty was to provide heirs."

The carriage pulled into the mews and entered the courtyard that was hidden from the road.

"Here we are, let me introduce you to my wife."

**

They entered the house through the back door and walked through to the drawing room. Inside Caroline was sitting in front of a window doing needlepoint. Hector lay at her feet until he saw Marty then bounded across the room to greet him.

"Good Lord, he is huge!" Pedro said and ruffled the big dog's head as he sniffed him.

"Hector is a Mastiff cross Dutch Shepherd. His father is retired now and spends his time sleeping."

There was a thud as the door was butted open and Troy walked in. He was old, his eyes had the silver sheen of cataracts, his muzzle and chest were grey and he was a bit deaf (especially when he chose to be).

He nuzzled Marty, who gave him a good petting, ignored Pedro and plonked himself down in the sunlight by Caroline.

"He is his father. His mother was almost twice Troy's size."

Pedro looked from one to the other.

"Troy? Hector? Aah, I see!"

"Martin?" Caroline said.

"Oh, yes, introductions. This is Caroline, my wife, Caroline, Dom Pedro, rightful king of Portugal."

"Lady Caroline, it is a pleasure to meet you."

Caroline stood and curtsied, Pedro bowed over her outstretched hand and kissed it.

"That's the formalities out of the way. Now I was on first name terms with your father. Can we continue the tradition?"

"Of course, I would be delighted to."

"I took the liberty of sending a coach for Maria, she should be here soon."

Pedro sat and asked Caroline, "You have children of your own?

"Four. Our eldest daughter Bethany is in Columbia with her husband who is an attaché to the British ambassador. Our eldest son James is a captain in the Royal Navy and is married with a son. Then there are the twins, Edwin is a lieutenant in the Horse Guards, his sister is in Newbury breeding horses."

They chatted about inconsequential things until Maria arrived.

"Bom dia, Papa. Hello, Milord Stockley," she said very seriously.

"Please call me Martin and my wife is Caroline." Marty smiled.

"How can you help us?" Pedro asked.

"Well, to start with we can organise transport for people who want to support you to Terceira. I would advise you to think about visiting France and the new king. There are more people there who would help form an army."

"What about weapons, an army is nothing if it is not armed."

"If you have funds, I think I can help with that as well."

Maria spoke up.

"We have been offered support by many people and are raising funds."

"Good then I will see to the procurement of muskets, swords and mobile artillery pieces. Powder and shot will also be needed."

"Are your generals experienced?" Caroline asked.

"A little but not in the type of warfare you fight in Europe," Pedro admitted.

"Then you will need some advisors." Marty smiled.

"My father talked about the advisors you provided to the guerillas during the French occupation."

Marty nodded.

"Some of the same men are still available now that the Greek war is all but over."

"I think Britain is very active in the world," Maria said.

Marty looked at her seriously.

"We try and influence things to go as we would wish without being seen to be directly involved. Politics in the wide world is sometimes a nasty business as you yourself are experiencing."

Maria looked at him seriously and said, "I am learning that what governments say is not necessarily what they do."

Pedro smiled at her, she was learning valuable lessons.

The Squadron of Evolution

James was recalled to London in early 1831 along with Admiral Codrington. He received his orders at the house Melissa had bought in Mount Street.

"Good Lord!"

Melissa looked at him curiously.

"What is it?"

"Me and my crew have been assigned to a new squadron and a new ship. According to my orders it is called The Squadron of Evolution that is an experimental squadron to evaluate new ship designs, weaponry, construction methods and propulsion against the traditional ones. I am to report to Admiral Codrington at Greenwich in two weeks."

"At least that is nearby." Melissa smiled.

There was the sound of a knock on the front door. Jules, their butler, opened the door to the drawing room and Caroline walked in.

"Good morning, my darlings," she said and kissed both of them.

"Mother, this is an unexpected pleasure," James said.

"Your father told me you had new orders. I swear there is nothing going on in the navy that he doesn't know about. He was typically obtuse about them and told me I would have to ask you if I wanted to know what they were."

James was amused, he knew his mother had an insatiable curiosity to the point of being downright nosey.

"So, you came straight around."

He handed her the letter and waited while she digested it. Melissa rang the bell for a servant and a young woman stepped into the room so quickly she must have anticipated the call.

"Ella, can you please get a tray of tea, the Earl Grey, and have Rose bring Martin down." She looked out of the window; it was a fine spring day. "We will take it to the gardens."

Like in a lot of upper class houses the baby was predominantly looked after by the nanny. Melissa breast fed him and spent time with him, but Rose looked after him the rest of the time. The gardens behind the house were more of a small, wooded park, Typical in that part of London where several houses would share a hidden garden, this one was larger than most.

Rose brought young Martin out in his baby carriage. A new innovation from America. The baby could sit or lay in the carriage which could be pushed by a person or pulled by a dog or goat-sized animal.

They sat by a table set up by the servants and Caroline poured the tea. They all took it black with lemon.

"I have some news as well. I have been asked to mentor Princess Alexandria Victoria."

Both Melissa and James were surprised.

"I thought she was under the thumb of her mother and that tyrant Conroy," James said.

"So they wish, but the young lady has a mind of her own and asked for me personally after meeting your father. I believe William may have had something to do with it."

"What are you to mentor her on?" Melissa asked.

"World affairs and politics. I am to sit with her every Tuesday afternoon for two hours."

"A position of influence," James said.

Caroline just smiled.

"Now, tell me what this Squadron of Evolution is all about."

James shrugged,

"You have read my orders; they arrived this morning, so you know as much as I."

"But why you?"

"Aah, now that is a different question. I wrote to the admiralty and volunteered to be part of any trials of steam ships, so I imagine this has something to do with that."

**

Janes reported to Codrington and met him in a temporary office.

"Captain Stockley, you are the first of three captains to join the squadron. The others will join us in Portsmouth."

James looked slightly confused.

"We are not to stay here?"

"No, unfortunately not. We need to be near the Royal Naval College and School of Naval Architecture, which is in Portsmouth."

"May I move my family there?"

"Up to you what you do. You will not get any allowance for it."

James smiled knowingly.

"No more than I expected, Sir. I will cover my own living costs."

"You have expressed an interest in steam and new weaponry, did you know your father has a pair of steam ships similar to that Sloop of Hastings?"

"I do, Sir. We discussed their merits and the experience his captains have had so far."

"Well, I want you to be objective. Report honestly on your experiences and findings, judge the ships on their merits not on your expectations."

"I will, Sir."

"Good, our first mission is to evaluate what is available. You will accompany me on a tour of shipyards that are constructing steam ships. We will also visit the engineering companies that are producing the engines and guns.

**

That evening when he got home, James talked to Melissa over dinner.

"I don't even have a ship! We will be travelling around the whole of the United Kingdom looking at construction methods and engineering works."

"Well at least you will be home more than when you are sailing."

"That's the next part. Once this tour is over in a month or six weeks I will be based in Portsmouth."

Melissa lent forward and put her hand on his.

"That's alright we can rent a house down there, close up this one and move everybody down there."

James sighed.

"I know Admiral Superintendent, Sir Frederick Maitland. I will write and ask if his staff can look for a suitable house."

As it turned out, the admiral knew of exactly the house that the young Captain needed. The outgoing commissioner, who he had replaced, had moved out of his house in the village of Fratton on Portsea Island. The house was furnished, large enough for their entire household and available for rent at a reasonable price. The other advantage was its view over Spithead.

While James set off on his tour, Melissa busied herself getting them moved. The baggage and people would be moved by carriage and box vans. The vans were enclosed wagons that would protect the baggage from the inclement British weather. The carriage for the staff was on loan from James's father. He and Melissa would travel in their landau.

**

James and Admiral Codrington rented a small steam ship to tour the shipyards. They started in London, working their way down the Thames. Their reception by some shipwrights was downright hostile, the mere mention of steam was enough to start the shipwright swearing and cursing. The fact they arrived in a steamboat even if it had a couple of masts was enough to set the traditionalists against them. Even the naval dockyards at Deptford, Woolwich, Chatham and Sheerness were reluctant to talk about steam and had no plans or ideas of how to build a steam ship.

"It seems that only the smaller yards are investing in steam and some in iron for framing and knees," James commented as they headed north up towards the River Tyne.

In Sunderland they found extensive shipyards as they expected including Austin and Sons and Thomas Haw. Both were experimenting with iron and steam but still predominantly building in wood. The Tyne builders were renowned for making ships to a price, which, in fact, was a side-line to properly building ships of the highest quality. Making ships was a fast way to put together a ship using the minimum of materials for the price. As the owners pointed out "you get what you pay for."

The Firth of Forth was next and then through the Union canal to Glasgow and the Clyde.

It took a while to get there but it was worth it. William McGill was building steamboats for river and sea and using iron in their construction. Denny's was another. The Scots were enthusiastic adopters of new technology and new shipbuilders were springing up all the time. They were also training new skills associated with iron working such as hot riveting and forging.

Their next stop was Belfast where Robert Hickson ran a shipyard on Dargan's Island. He had vision and enthusiasm but no capital. While Belfast was destined to become a major centre of shipbuilding Hickson was not the man to do it. Then it was on to Bristol.

George Hilhouse and Company had constructed the Albion, a paddle steamer which operated between Bristol and Ireland. They and the other shipwrights of Bristol benefited from their close proximity to

Cornwall, where steam engine development was progressing at a pace, and were building East Indiamen and West Indiamen.

Next stop was Cornwall to visit Harvey & Co and the Copperhouse Foundry to look at engines. The chief designer had just gotten back from London and was full of the news about the two new ships for Admiral Stockley.

**

Their final stop was, of course, Portsmouth. They docked and James was informed that his wife had rented a house just a mile or so away. As they had arrived late in the evening he got a coach to take him to the house.

Melissa greeted him warmly and after dinner the two had an early night. Absence makes the heart grow fonder, and also increases the libido. Neither got much sleep that night.

In the morning, he walked to the navy yard and found the squadron's offices. Codrington greeted him.

"Good morning, James. I hope you are rested, we will be visiting the college today."

James had been looking forward to this. While having attended the college for three years and had the regular naval officer's grounding in mathematics and navigation, he was lacking in engineering knowledge and wanted to improve. The Royal School had been a separate institution then and had only merged with the college in 1826. They walked to the entrance in College Road and met Lieutenant Governor, Captain John Wentworth Loring.

"We produce the best-educated officers in the navy and they are looked over in favour of officers with sea time and connections," he complained.

"I was here for three years," James said, "I graduated in '16 just before the merger."

"You did? What was your name again?" Loring obviously had a poor memory.

"Stockley. James Stockley."

"James Stockley, that name rings a bell, now where have I seen it?"

He suddenly sat upright.

"Admiral Stockley's son! Your name is on the list of captains of the school."

James tried to look modest. Codrington smiled; he knew James's record.

"Well, you must be introduced to the boys. You are a fine example of what a graduate from here can achieve."

James had never thought of himself as a role model but if this was the price, then he would pay it.

Codrington was thinking along the same lines.

"Sir, before we go off to do that, I should mention that we are here to learn about the latest thinking in naval architecture and construction. Is there someone whose brains we can pick?"

"We can ask the master, Reverend Inman. He is head of Naval Architecture. "

With that he jumped up and led them out. They visited classes and were introduced. James had to tell the story of his career over and over again.

"I left school and came straight here. This was better and more relevant to what I wanted to do. When I graduated, I was offered a lieutenant's position, but that would have meant being the sixth on a first rate. I chose to stay a mid and go onto a frigate where I would see some action. I eventually became First on a marine landing ship and took part in amphibious landings."

A hand shot up.

"Yes? You have a question?"

"Were you ever wounded, Sir?"

"Several times. None so serious that stitches couldn't close them."

This would elicit OOOHs and AAAHs.

"An officer must expect to lead his men by example and be at the forefront of a boarding or a land attack. You need to know how to fight as well as run a ship."

Another hand went up.

"Yes?"

"Have you ever been sunk, Sir?"

"Once in the Java Sea. The ship was hit by a waterspout and driven on to a reef. We lost half the men before we were rescued."

More OOHs and AAHs and questions.

They finally got to the master's office. Reverend Inman was at a huge blackboard working on a complex mathematical problem. They waited until he stopped. Loring coughed and Reverend Inman turned around to see who was in his office. He peered at the three of them and focussed on James.

"My Gad! Is that young Stockley?"

"Hello, Master." James stepped forward to shake his hand.

"What are you doing back here?" Inman said, then noticed his epaulette. "A captain now?"

"I am and this is Admiral Codrington, my superior in The Squadron of Evolution."

"What's that? Never heard of it."

Codrington stepped forward.

"It is a new squadron to test new naval architectures, propulsion and armaments."

"About time too, the French are ahead of us," Inman stated flatly.

"We would like to know more of the college's work on architectures."

Inman stood and started for the door saying, "Let me show you something."

They followed him to a shed built in the courtyard of the college. Inside was a large tank of water, students were around it and appeared to be playing with model boats.

Inman spoke as if lecturing a class.

"The shape of a ship's hull is fundamental to its efficiency and hasn't changed much in the last two hundred years and will not if the duffers in the navy have their way. Traditional ships have bluff bows and need a tumblehome to allow for guns. Below the waterline they are slimmer than the decks but still bulge out."

He picked up a model of a traditional frigate hull and handed it to Codrington.

"If you want to use the least power to push a ship through the water then the ideal shape is long and thin. However, that makes it hard to steer as a long thin ship will always want to go in a straight line. So what we are looking for here are hull shapes that are efficient, stable and allow for steering and the mounting of engines."

"How do you test the idea with a model?" James asked.

"Testing for speed is easy. We attach a line to the bow of the model and tow it through the water with a set of weights." He showed them a set of pulleys at the end of the tank and the weights that hung from the cords that ran over them.

Inman barked some instructions to the boys who set up three models at the other end of the tank.

"We will use the same amount of weight to pull each of them. Now watch."

He signalled to the boys who let the models go. One was notably faster while the frigate model came second, and a fat merchantman came last.

"This shape," Inman said on retrieving the winner, "is the most hydrodynamically efficient. It has a sharper, more sloping bow, is narrower at the waterline while her upper hull has flatter sides. This is a good shape for a ship propelled by side wheels."

James asked the question that had been burning in his mind.

"May I attend an architectural class?"

Inman smiled at him.

"Your mathematics was always good; I think you could cope with it. Yes, that would be in order."

**

James and Melissa settled into their house, and he went back to school. Luckily the classes were only on Tuesday afternoons, Wednesday and Thursday mornings which left him time to work with Codrington and the other captains.

Codrington had recruited three young captains who were technically capable. While James was interested in hull design, Simon Stafford was an engineer at heart and their engine specialist and Archibald Atherton was their gunnery expert.

New hull forms were commissioned and tested against traditional designs. It annoyed them all that they had to get the hulls built by civilian firms as the master shipwrights in the royal dockyards wanted nothing to do with them. But build them they did and soon they took delivery of a cutter-sized ship called the Paddy which had been originally built in Cork. They lengthened her hull in a shipyard in the Hamble to meet the ratio of length to beam required by the college.

The steam frigate Firebrand was built in Merchant's Yard in Limehouse and was one hundred and fifty-five feet three inches long and twenty-six feet five inches at the beam. Propelled by side wheels and two masts she was fitted with a Butterley and Co. one hundred and forty Nominal Horsepower, (NHP), side beam twin-cylinder engine. James captained her.

The third new ship was a brig called the Aspen. Built in Hamble she was longer and narrower than traditional brigs. All three ships with two more sailing frigates and a second rate were sent to the Belgian coast where the French were supporting the Belgians in their war against the Dutch. The aim being to persuade the French to withdraw their squadron.

**

At the beginning of '32 Codrington was replaced by Sir Pulleney Malcom and he had the French and Spanish fleets off of Belgium under his command. During his time in command more trials took place.

The Paddy was the size of a cutter and would serve to compare the performance of a traditional hull against the new design. They challenged the tender of HMS Victory, a renowned fast ship, to a race and the challenge was taken up in July '32 off the Irish coast.

James had the honour of captaining the Paddy and the course was designed by Inman to compare the handling as well. James had a crew of experienced sailors who he had practised well, and there would be a running start across a line between two buoys. The course was over ten miles and involved sailing with the wind coming from all angles to the hull.

They started off with a downwind leg and as soon as they crossed the starting line set all sail. The Paddy built up an early lead, gradually pulling ahead. James had the wheel himself and looked across at the Emerald as they overtook her. Her captain was the eighth lieutenant on the Victory, Victor Monroe. James raised his hat. Men ran forward and started to wet the Emeralds sails. They gained maybe a quarter of a knot and slowed the rate the Paddy was overtaking them a little.

They approached the first turn and James called the orders.

"Standby to tack to port, ready the jib, trimmers to their stations!"

They got to the buoy and with a two-length lead he could turn as he wanted.

"Ready! NOW!"

He spun the wheel, and the foremast men pulled the jib around to add its power to the turn pushing the bow around. The trimmers hauled the square sails around as the wind came on their beam. It was a perfectly executed manoeuvre and they took off along that leg. The Emerald also made a near perfect turn and was in hot pursuit, but the lead lengthened.

This leg was three miles and as they got to the buoy they had stretched their lead to around four minutes. The next leg was into the wind and they sailed as close to it as they could which was at least five degrees closer than the Emerald could sail. The advantage in speed plus the reduced distance they had to sail saw them make the next turn eight minutes ahead.

The last leg had the wind on their starboard quarter and the Paddy flew.

"This is her best angle to the wind," James crowed as they raced towards the finish line. The Victory marked one end of it and she fired a gun as they crossed. He had his watch in his hand as the Emerald crossed and they fired a gun for her.

"Twelve minutes! That's a bloody mile faster."

Determined to regain face, a second race was scheduled by the admiralty for August to be held off the Scilly Islands. The result, in very different sea conditions, was almost the same.

**

The admiralty was determined not to change. Led by a board of ageing admirals they persisted in trying to disprove Symonds designs. Change would take time

The Heir Presumptive

Caroline went to Kensington Palace to join Princess Alexandria Victoria and her mother the Duchess of Kent and Strathearn. There she met and took an instant dislike to Sir John Ponsonby Conroy. He was the duchess's comptroller, her chief accountant. Caroline immediately sensed that there was more to their relationship than met the eye.

The princess, who liked to be called Victoria, was a melancholy child trapped in an overprotective world by her overbearing mother and Sir John, who seemed to have an unusual amount of power where the young princess was concerned. Caroline decided she would bring some light into the child's life.

Victoria's life was strictly regimented. Morning lessons began at a half past nine sharp and covered Greek, Latin, Italian, French and German for two hours. They would resume at three with decorum, reading and Caroline's hour. Lessons ended at five. She was isolated from other children and her every move monitored and recorded

Even with all of that, Caroline found a strong-willed young lady who was building up a head of resentment towards her mother and her advisor. The trip to the Malvern Hills did nothing to change that. Caroline wrote to Marty.

The trip to the Malvern Hills is akin to the tours the old kings of England took. They descend on the country houses of the aristocracy and wealthy and parade Victoria as if she were already queen. I found out that they had released the planned route with its timing in advance

of our departure so that people would line the streets of the towns we pass through. Victoria's melancholy only deepens the further we go.

What Caroline did about it was to make sure that she spent more time with Victoria than just her lessons and become her confidant. Her rank of Countess was enough to keep Sir John at bay especially after their first confrontation.

"Lady Caroline, you are to restrict your contact with the princess to the hour's lesson a day," Sir John told her after a servant reported that the two were talking outside of lesson time.

Caroline looked at him coldly, her eyes flat grey.

"You presume to tell me what I can and cannot do? Do I have to remind you who I am?"

He was not quailed.

"You will conform to the system."

"Oh, I will, will I? Shall we discuss your nocturnal wanderings, Sir John?

The man took a step back. She closed in relentlessly.

"You may be able to bully and badger a young girl, but you will not bully me. And before you think that you can get the duchess to send me away, let me warn you that my husband would take great pleasure in challenging you to a duel and carving out your heart when I tell him you came to my chamber with ill intentions."

He had in fact knocked on her door late the first night in a strange house in the mistaken belief that it was the duchess's.

"Then there is the small fact that you and the duchess are lovers. What would the king say if the scandal sheets found out you were humping the duchess and had it all over their front pages?"

The door opened and the duchess came in. Caroline curtsied and smiled, no trace of the previous conversation visible at all.

"There you are, John. What have you two been talking about?"

"Sir John was just telling me that he approves of me spending some time with Victoria to increase her knowledge of the world."

She smiled sweetly at him.

**

Caroline and the princess sat next to each other in the coach as they travelled the toll road towards Oxford. They passed through Beaconsfield where small crowds waved and cheered. Then they arrived at High Wycombe.

"This town was famous for paper making over the last two centuries but then the making of cloth became its main industry. Nowadays the making of furniture is prevalent especially that of Windsor Chairs," Caroline told the Princess.

The duchess snorted in contempt.

"Why does a princess need to know of common trade?"

"Because the empire that she will inherit is built on it. Without trade Britain is just another island. With our navy and our trade worldwide, our empire is sustained," Caroline replied.

Victoria noticed that her mother was developing an active dislike of Countess Caroline, which made her like the lady even more.

Crowds cheered and bunting flapped in the wind but even though she smiled and waved back Victoria found the whole thing very trying and tiring. They stayed that night at West Wycombe Park, the home of Sir John Dashwood-King Fourth Baronet. He was a Tory member of parliament who represented the borough of Wycombe and opposed the Reform Bill.

After dinner that evening while Victoria and Caroline sat doing needlepoint Victoria asked, "What is the Reform Bill they were talking about over dinner?"

Caroline answered carefully as they were being attended to by one of the duchess's servants.

"It is a proposal by the liberals to change the electoral system by reapportioning the constituencies and standardising the property qualifications to vote."

"Who can vote now?"

"Anyone who owns property in a borough."

"Can a woman vote?"

Caroline smiled at her,

"My you are full of questions this evening. At the moment it is not accepted that a woman votes even if she has property but there is no legal bar. However, the Reform Bill explicitly excludes women from voting."

"What do you think of it?" Victoria asked.

Caroline switched to French, ostensibly to give the young princess some practice but really to conceal what was said from the servant.

"Martin and I control five boroughs in Cheshire and two in Dorset. One of those boroughs has a dozen legitimate voters, one of which is the member of parliament. The others vary from a few hundred voters to a few thousand. The Bill would change the voting landscape completely making the government more answerable to the people than just a few large landowners. It will especially affect large cities like Manchester and Birmingham."

"You would lose power?"

"I would on paper but there is more to power than that. Influence is more important. Every government has an agenda which it tries to push through in its term. Up to now the Tories have been in power for a very long time and want to preserve the status quo. The Whigs will probably win the election as the pressure from the public has grown and they want the reforms the Bill proposes. We have seen riots and demonstrations all around the country. From our perspective as influencers the difference is that the Tories want things to stay the same. The country needs to evolve but the Whigs want change quickly therefore we must rein them in, so that the change is gradual."

**

Blenheim Palace was their next stop after passing through Oxford where huge crowds gathered. Victoria was showing signs of fatigue, but her mother would not hear of returning home or slowing down the tour. They stayed at Blenheim Palace, the home of George Spencer-Churchill, the sixth Duke of Marlborough. Another Tory member of parliament representing Woodstock.

The duke regaled the princess with his family history and opposition to 'any bloody reforms that put power into the hands of the proletariat.'

Victoria complained of a headache and went to bed early. Caroline sat with Lady Jane, the Duchess of Marlborough that evening.

"My husband is a bore, regaling poor Princess Victoria like that."

"All the Tories are agitated. They can see themselves losing power for the first time in fifty years."

"Where does your husband stand in all this?

"Martin? He is not a political animal but if anything, he is a liberal at heart."

Lady Jane was silent for a while, her hands busy as her needle dipped in and out of the sampler she was embroidering.

"Is your husband faithful?"

Caroline knew where this was going as the duke was known for his affairs.

"He is."

"How do you know? He was a sailor and away so much of the time."

Caroline put down her needle.

"Martin and I have a relationship that is rooted in love. I am devoted to him as he is to me."

Jane kept sewing as she asked.

"But you must have been approached by many handsome men while he was away?"

"I have and some needed to learn the hard way that I was not interested. My behaviour before I met Martin is to blame for that."

Jane giggled "You did have quite the reputation."

"Indeed," Caroline said and picked up her needle again. She concentrated on her sewing, then asked,

"Have you been approached?"

Jane blushed, giving herself away.

"I have. A most handsome man."

"Do not be fooled by flatterers. What would your husband do if he found out?"

Jane thought for a moment.

"He would probably kill him for the sake of honour."

"Just as Martin did for me when we first met."

"He did? Oh! I remember now, I was only sixteen when that happened."

"I was eighteen and he was sixteen."

They sat in companionable silence then chatted about inconsequential matters until Caroline said, "I am for bed. We will be sat in that damn coach for most of tomorrow." She stopped at the door. "Whatever you decide to do, do not let him take advantage of you. Stay in charge of the affair at all times and if you can't, let me know and I will help you."

Jame had the thought from Caroline's tone that she meant something more than just advice.

**

The next day they were approaching Whittington Court where they proposed to overnight when Caroline noticed a man pacing the coach in the adjacent fields on what looked like a farm horse. He had no saddle and the bridle looked like one for carting. She also noticed he carried what could be a fowling piece or a musket.

She watched as he paced them for a mile when all of a sudden, he kicked the horse into a run and got ahead of them. Alarm bells went off in her head and she put her hand through the hidden pocket in her dress and clutched the butt of her revolver.

"Victoria, dear. Please lay down on the seat." She pushed her over.

"What on earth?" the duchess squawked.

"I say!" Sir John exclaimed as she drew her pistol and knelt at the window.

"Shut up and get down. I think there is a man with a gun."

To give him credit Sir John laid his body across the duchess to protect her.

Caroline scanned the hedge to the side of the road and spotted the horse tied to a tree. She rapidly scanned for the man and saw his head above a small mound, the gun pointing at the coach.

She fired, cocked, fired, cocked and fired again. The bullets throwing up dirt in front of the man's face. His gun went off and then they were past.

"Keep moving!" Caroline shouted at the driver.

At Whittington house Sir John took her to task.

"What the hell were you thinking? And why do you have a gun?"

"We were attacked."

"We only have your word for that, I saw nothing."

Caroline took him by the arm and led him to the carriage.

"What do you think that is?" She pointed to a hole above the door.

"My god."

Caroline wrote a message to Marty in their private code and asked for it to be sent to London by fast courier. The horseman would change horses every ten miles and be in London in a few hours. Then she met the duchess and Sir John in private.

"Do you agree this should not be made public?"

"We do. It is unthinkable that someone should try and kill the future queen."

"Good, I have informed my husband who will inform the Prime Minister. I am sure he will track down the individual and make sure he is no longer a threat."

"Lord Martin is known for his… efficiency," Sir John said.

The duchess pursed her lips.

"We will keep you on for a while. You can provide Victoria with a measure of discreet protection."

Caroline looked at her coldly.

"We will see what Martin says about that. He may have someone else in mind."

Epilogue

Martin sat with the Prime Minister and Wellington discussing the recent attempt on the young princess's life.

"Have you brought your investigation to an end?" Wellington asked.

"We have, the culprit was found at his father's farm. He was the younger of two sons and had been recently attending some rabble rousers speeches about the Reform Act. He was blaming the king for not forcing the government to adopt the bill and our young revolutionary took it upon himself to send a message."

"Where is he now?" Grey asked.

"In a bedlam for the insane in Yorkshire," Marty said grimly.

"His parents?"

"Will not say a word. They are royalists through and through and the boy's actions are a complete embarrassment."

"So happy to keep it quiet?" Wellington said.

"Absolutely."

"What about the staff?" Grey asked as he spooned sugar into tea,

Marty and Wellington sipped their coffee.

"Sworn to secrecy. We don't want anybody else to get the same idea."

Grey was not finished.

"And the rabble rouser?"

"Disappeared," Marty smiled. "No one has seen hide nor hair of him."

"Hmpph," Wellington grunted, "Caroline is staying with her?"

"Along with Lark."

"Aah, the tuneful young agent from Abergavenny." Wellington smiled.

Marty took a biscuit from the plate in the middle of the table.

"Crack shot and a demon with a knife as well as an excellent music teacher."

"What about Portugal?" Grey asked.

"Developing. Several ships are on lease to the Portuguese Liberal Association to take anyone who wants to go to join their army. So far there are as many British and French as there are Portuguese."

"Good, what we need now is some kind of incident to push the French into intervening," Wellington said.

Marty sat back and looked, not smug, but confident.

"I will leave it in your hands." Wellington then reached for a brandy bottle and a trio of snifter glasses.

"Anyone for a brandy?"

Authors Notes

Ricin is a poison derived from the beans of the castor plant and is a by-product of making castor oil. It can be a liquid, powder, or crystals. There is no antidote and ingesting it causes symptoms not unlike food poisoning including vomiting and bloody diarrhoea. One milligram in food can kill an adult person.

The Battle of Navarino actually occurred much as I wrote it here in the story. The only change I made was to replace Admiral Codrington with Marty. Codrington was a supporter of Hellenic Independence, a member of the London Philhellenic Committee, and no diplomat. The diplomat of the three admirals was Henri de Rigny and Codrington despised that quality in the man. Codrington was a popular hero in England for his role in Trafalgar but it remains a mystery to me why, when the government wanted the Treaty to be enforced and to avoid conflict, they would put such a man in charge. The fall out as the Russians declared war on the Ottomans saw the blame land squarely on Codrington's shoulders as this was the outcome the British did not want. He was never given another operational command and spent the next ten years defending his actions.

Estimates of the actual size of the Ottoman fleet vary widely and for the sake of the story I have used the largest. The smallest estimate of their effective strength put it at just thirty-six ships.

In 1928 the Egyptians left Greece but it took until 1929 for the Ottomans to finally leave and then only with the Russian army camped on the sultan's doorstep.

Orangeism is a reference to The Loyal Orange Institution in Northern Ireland associated with the Protestant Association.

The Danubian Principalities were a common term for what is now Moldavia and Wallachia.

Robert Hickson's shipyard in Belfast was bought by Edward Harland in 1858 and then formed a partnership with Gustav Wolff and in 1861 Harland and Wolff was born.

The eldest son of an Earl is entitled to the Earl's previous title which in the case of Marty was Viscount.

Glossary of sailing terms used in this book

Beam – The **beam** of a ship is its width at its widest point

Bowsprit – a spar projecting from the bow of a vessel, especially a sailing vessel, used to carry the headstay as far forward as possible.

Cable – a cable length or length of cable is a nautical unit of measure equal to one tenth of a nautical mile or approximately 100 fathoms. Owing to anachronisms and varying techniques of measurement, a cable length can be anywhere from 169 to 220 metres, depending on the standard used. In this book we assume 200 yards.

Cay – a low bank or reef of coral, rock, or sand especially one on the islands in Spanish America.

Futtock shrouds – are rope, wire or chain links in the rigging of a traditional square-rigged ship. They run from the outer edges of a top downwards and inwards to a point on the mast or lower shrouds, and carry the load of the shrouds that rise from the edge of the top. This prevents any tendency of the top itself to tilt relative to the mast.

Gripe – to tend to come up into the wind in spite of the helm.

Ketch – a two-masted sailing vessel, fore-and-aft rigged with a tall mainmast and a mizzen stepped forward of the rudderpost.

Knee – is a natural or cut, curved piece of wood.[1] Knees, sometimes called ships knees, are a common form of bracing in boatbuilding.

A Nautical Mile is 1.151 statute miles or 1/60th of a degree of latitude at the equator.

Leeway – the leeward drift of a ship i.e. with the wind towards the lee side.

Loblolly boys – Surgeon's' assistants

Lugger – a sailing vessel defined by its rig using the lug sail on all of its one or several masts. They were widely used as working craft, particularly off the coast. Luggers varied extensively in size and design. Many were undecked, open boats. Others were fully decked.

Mizzen – 1. on a yawl, ketch or dandy the after mast.
    2. (on a vessel with three or more masts) the third mast from the bow.

Pawls – a catch that drops into the teeth of a capstan to stop it being pulled in reverse.

In ordinary – vessels "in ordinary" (from the 17th century) are those out of service for repair or maintenance, a meaning coming over time to cover a reserve fleet or "mothballed" ships.

Ratlines – are lengths of thin line tied between the shrouds of a sailing ship to form a ladder. Found on all square-rigged ships, whose crews must go aloft to stow the square sails, they also appear on larger fore-and-aft rigged vessels to aid in repairs aloft or conduct a lookout from above.

Rib – a thin strip of pliable timber laid athwarts inside a hull from inwale to inwale at regular close intervals to reinforce its planking. Ribs differ from frames or futtocks in being far smaller dimensions and bent in place compared to frames or futtocks, which are normally sawn to shape, or natural crooks that are shaped to fit with an adze, axe or chisel.

Sea anchor – any device, such as a bucket or canvas funnel, dragged in the water to keep a vessel heading into the wind or reduce drifting.

Shrouds – on a sailing boat, the shrouds are pieces of standing rigging which hold the mast up from side to side. There is frequently more than one shroud on each side of the boat. Usually, a shroud will connect at the top of the mast, and additional shrouds might connect partway down the mast, depending on the design of the boat. Shrouds terminate at their bottom ends at the chain plates, which are tied into the hull. They are sometimes held outboard by channels, a ledge that keeps the shrouds clear of the gunwales.

Stay – is part of the standing RIGGING and is used to support the weight of a mast. It is a large strong rope extending from the upper end of each mast.

Sweeps – another name for oars.

Tack – if a sailing ship is tacking or if the people in it tack it, it is sailing towards a particular point in a series of lateral movements rather than in a direct line.

Tumblehome – a hull which grows narrower above the waterline than its beam.

Wear ship – to change the tack of a sailing vessel, especially a square-rigger, by coming about so that the wind passes astern.

Weather Gauge – sometimes spelled weather gauge is the advantageous position of a fighting sailing vessel relative to another. It is also known as "nautical gauge" as it is related to the seashore.

And now

An Excerpt from Lady Bethany Book 2, Betrayal.

Clean Up

The Right Honourable Bethany Stockley; tall, elegant, beautiful, and educated, codename Chaton and known in these parts as Rosa Collins. Crouched in the filth at the back of a cantina in Veracruz dressed as a beggar woman with filthy hair and ragged dirty clothes. To all the world she looked as if she was searching the rubbish for something to eat, but she was intently listening to a conversation between two men in a backroom.

One of the men, a Columbian, was forcefully making a point.

"I want the names and cargo of the ships. Your agent has the lists of sailings, and you will copy it for me."

"But, Senior López, he keeps it in the safe now that Senior Luna was killed."

Beth knew all about that, she had killed him and left the warning on his body. He had been selling the list to the Columbian privateers and had been caught red handed when he tried to sell it to Beth. The authorities had been outraged and were looking for his murderer. She had been interviewed as she was ostensibly American and the current list had American ships on it, but they had no evidence and had to let her go.

López didn't care about that.

"You will get me the list, or your family will suffer. That's a very pretty girl you have, she would fetch a good price on the block."

Rivera caved in.

"I will get it, please do not hurt my family."

"I want it by Friday."

Beth had heard enough and scuttled away, dragging a foot as if disabled. Once she was clear of the cantina, she resumed walking normally and headed back to the house they used as a base in Veracruz. Manuela, the resident agent, opened the door and grinned at the sight of her. Beth looked at her inquiringly as something was obviously up, but the urge to get clean overcame her curiosity and she stepped past her into the dim interior.

She immediately sensed another presence, and her hand went to the karambit dagger hidden in her sash. Then she caught the scent of tar and man. She let her eyes adjust, it was Richard, the captain of her schooner, the Fox. He wrinkled his nose as she stepped closer,

"Pee-uw, you stink."

"I know it's part of my charm.'

"We have a communication from London. Came in on a merchant ship."

"What does it say?"

"No idea it's in code, but there is a second envelope from Seb."

Beth rolled her eyes, "I will look at it after I am clean. Give me the letter."

"Good, because the smell is making me gag."

Beth poked her tongue out at him as she went into the back room where she knew a tub of hot water was waiting. She stripped and sank into it. The letter from Sebastian, her betrothed, told her of some of the goings on of her family in Burma where her father was the British ambassador. Most of the things he told her were mundane but a section that was encoded gave her details of the undercover operations. She cried a little when he said it could be months before they saw each other again.

**

Bathed and dressed in a typical Mexican skirt and blouse she sat down at the kitchen table to decode the message. It was from Admiral Turner, the head of Military Intelligence, overseas.

American's happy with progress so far. They have identified a Columbian who calls himself El Dragon who is targeting their ships. Stop him.

M is still in Asia, do not expect them home soon. Lancelot sends his love.

Contact in Columbia is Lucifer, you can find him in Cartagena at a cantina called La Orquídea Morada.

It went on to give recognition phrases and more details. She wondered about El Dragon. Was he López? But then she thought that López would call himself the Wolf, no, it wouldn't be that easy. Richard was still waiting so she told him the news.

"So, they have a name and that's it?" he sniffed unimpressed.

"That's about it. Why don't you and the crew keep a weatherly ear out for any mention of him. If he has gotten the attention of the Americans, he must be quite active."

Richard rose to leave.

"Will do boss."

Manuela sat opposite Beth and rested her hands on the table.

"I have not heard of this Dragon. He is not based here."

"It would be too easy if he was."

Printed in Great Britain
by Amazon

42984904R00162